VET

A S

The dog and I gazed at one another. He was showing too much of the whites of his eyes. A hysterical dog? I certainly didn't want a problem pup. But what beautiful, large eyes! What an awful coat though! The animal, which should have been thickly covered in silky hair, was half naked. And he wasn't really black and tan; rather a blackish brown and cream. The poor state of his coat apart, his markings were nice; pale gold paws, cream shirt-front, pale gold lower half of face contrasting well with dark upper half, small gold circles above the eyes, round gold ear rings on the cheeks.

I got down on the floor. 'Kimmy. . .nice dog. Come here. . .come on.' The tail, which should have been a proud plume but was a thin rat's tail, wagged; tentatively.

Suddenly I saw a louse wander slowly from the middle of the dog's head to his left ear. . .

Also by Alex Duncan in *Star*

IT'S A VET'S LIFE
THE VET HAS NINE LIVES
VETS IN THE BELFRY
VETS IN CONGRESS
VET AMONG THE PIGEONS
THE BEST OF VETS

VET'S CHOICE

The Story of Sir Timothy Hemjoy and his People

Alex Duncan

STAR

A STAR BOOK
published by
The Paperback Division of
W. H. ALLEN & Co. Ltd

A Star Book
Published in 1978
by the Paperback Division of
W. H. Allen & Co. Ltd.
A Howard and Wyndham Company
44 Hill Street, London W1X 8LB

Printed in Great Britain by
The Anchor Press Ltd Tiptree, Essex
ISBN 0 352 30218 6

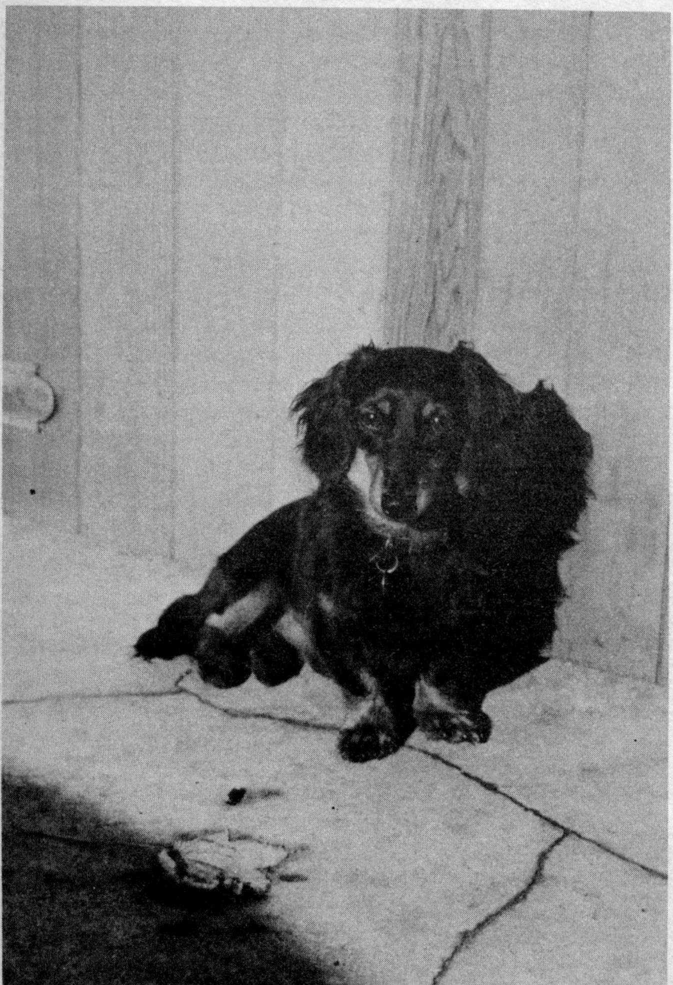

Pedigree Certificate

NAME OF DOG HEMJOY SIR TIMOTHY (KIM.) K.C. REGISTRATION No. 10105/63

BREED MINIATURE LONG HAIRED DACHSHUND SEX DOG COLOUR BLACK & TAN DATE OF BIRTH MAY 1 1962.

BREEDER MRS C.E. HEMMINGS BREEDER'S ADDRESS CHURCHMANS FARM POUND LANE HURST.

OWNER .... OWNER'S ADDRESS ....

SIRE (1)	GRAND SIRE (3)	GREAT GRAND SIRE (7)
NAME HEMJOY BROWN: BOY K.C. REGISTRATION No. 94420/56 OWNER MRS HEMMINGS ADDRESS	SPRINGMOUNT QUEST	CH SPRINGMOUNT MADRIGAL
		GREAT GRAND DAM (8) PRIORSGATE CHRISTINA
	GRAND DAM (4) HEMJOY JEMINA	GREAT GRAND SIRE (9) HEMJOY ROBERT
		GREAT GRAND DAM (10) ADRELSON JOYFUL JENNIFER.
DAM (2)	GRAND SIRE (5)	GREAT GRAND SIRE (11)
NAME FORESTWAY LOTTE K.C. REGISTRATION No. 49218/59 OWNER MRS HEMMINGS ADDRESS	PRIORSGATE JOSEPH	CH PRIORSGATE MARLENWOOD ROYCE
		GREAT GRAND DAM (12) PRIORSGATE CHRISTMAS DAY.
	GRAND DAM (6) RADIANT OF FORESTWAY	GREAT GRAND SIRE (13) CH BADGERSWOOD MARTIN VON WALDER
		GREAT GRAND DAM (14) HONEY OF FORESTWAY.

Date ....

Signed C. E. Hemmings

Address Churchmans Farm Pound Lane Hurst.

SPILLERS LIMITED supply these Pedigree Forms as part of their service. but can accept no responsibility for any transaction involved in their use.

DECISIONS

Any Veterinary Surgeon who deals with pets hears a good many owners' life stories, especially from the old and the lonely. As the conscientious general practitioner — using every means to arrive at the correct diagnosis — will listen to his patients, so the vet must listen to learn.

Even an owner who cares deeply for his pet can be responsible for the animal's ailments by providing the wrong food or environment. An old man, who'd owned labradors in the country, now lives in a small city flat with a grossly over-weight dog of the same breed. The owner, disabled by arthritis, can't give the dog the necessary exercise and in turn the dog's health suffers. That is just one obvious example of the interrelation of animal and owner. Such interrelations can be harmful or pleasurable and rewarding for both, usually depending less on the animal than the owner.

In some cases where one searches for the relevant links between animal and owner the inevitable questions come into one's mind; *what has made Mrs Snooks select a particular kind of pet? Why an alsatian rather than a poodle? Why a dachshund and not a labrador*?

Owners, who deliberately go for a particular breed, can usually give a positive reason and behind the reason there is always a story.

I was collecting such owners' stories for a book, convinced that the subject was fascinating, when a writer — virtually my alter ego — answered the central question more fully than most.

Madelaine could not have given pat, immediate reasons for wanting a certain breed of dog. Her motives did not emerge until later. But when her husband, Alex, asked her what she would like for her birthday she told him — without hesitation — that she wanted a long-haired miniature dachshund. Neither Madelaine nor Alex had ever owned a dog. Madelaine's sudden request seemed to come out of the blue.

'A dog? You can't be serious.' Her husband gazed at her as if she were one of his patients — with that quiet attentiveness that made them happy to describe their symptoms. 'What on earth would you want a dog for?'

She couldn't say *for protection* because they had nothing to protect. They were living in a small cottage, in a small garden, in a mellow and law-abiding Sussex village. Well, why did Madelaine want a dog? Not for protection; not because she was lonely, bored or emotionally frustrated. She obviously couldn't think of a sensible answer, and Alex was accustomed to sensible answers from her.

'It would be nice to have an animal around the place,' she answered, weakly.

'Who'd look after the dog when you go to London?' asked Alex. 'You don't imagine I'd take a dog to the hospital . . . have him sniffing around the consulting room while I'm seeing patients, do you?'

'I've thought about it. He wouldn't be a nuisance to you. I promise.'

We had been strolling in the garden. Alex stopped to examine the climbing roses which were covering the whole front of the cottage. The August heat had frizzled the blooms to parchment. 'If you want more roses you'd better cut the dead ones.'

She knew his ploy all too well. 'Don't change the subject. It's dogs we're discussing.'

'Aren't there enough dogs in our lane?'

As if to prove Alex's point the regular evening march-past was approaching their garden gate; Miss J. with six or eight long-haired dachshunds swirling about her legs. From the porch we watched them trot down the sun-dappled country lane towards the cricket field; red dachses, black and tans, large ones and miniatures, their plumed tails fluttering like the pennants on Brighton seafront.

'See that one?' Madelaine pointed out a coffee-coloured

miniature with dancing hind legs. 'That's what I want.'

'Not a lapdog! If you must have a pet, why not something sensible like a labrador?'

'Dachses are not lapdogs. If we had a dachs he'd get rid of the moles which are ruining your lawn. Digging . . . that's what those muscular shoulders are for.'

'There must be simpler ways of getting rid of moles.'

'You don't like poisoning animals.'

'Err . . . well . . . what's wrong with labradors?'

'Too big to carry. A dachs could go with me when I have to go to London.'

'I suppose so.' Alex was half convinced that he wouldn't be expected to take the dog to the hospital. 'But it's no good anyway. You've left it too late. I couldn't possibly find the kind of pup you want in time for your birthday.' He was using Madelaine's own rule against her. 'It's you who always insists that a gift must arrive on the right day.'

'I'd like to try all the same.'

'For a dachs on August twenty-first?'

'Yes.'

'Puppies don't grow on trees.'

'No. But if I find the right pup, may I have it?'

'Sure.' Alex looked confident. 'You won't, of course . . . not inside a week . . .'

'Thank you.'

'Wouldn't a labrador be a better idea?' for him the discussion had become comfortably academic. 'They seem good-natured brutes.'

'No, thank you.'

'A fluffy dachs or nothing?'

'A dachs or nothing.'

'I dare say you know why.'

I asked, '*Do* you know why?'

'Yes.'

That's how it began. Madelaine and her dog was to be one of the stories in my book *The Owners Animals Own.* But somehow that didn't work out. As the story unfolded it became clear to me that I was faced with a choice. Was the story to be included in my collection or should it — as a most unusual case — stand on its own? I chose the latter. Madelaine, a highly professional author, knew best how to tell this personal tale of interrelated animal and human lives. And in the end it was written exactly as she told it, beginning with the night after she had told her husband what she wanted for her birthday.

CHAPTER ONE

That night Alex slept peacefully, confident that he had averted the advent of an interloper. I lay awake, haunted by his ironical remark that I undoubtedly knew why I wanted a small dachshund. It worried me that I didn't know. Yet, as far as I could remember, I had never chosen a present capriciously.

Nor was I dissatisfied with what I had. I was grateful for the beautiful sight of the moonlight outlining the black bulk of the Sussex Downs, for the scent of roses and cut grass, for the familiar night-sounds of hedgehogs and owls.

It occurred to me that I'd never owned an animal. On my grandparents' estate in Lower Austria there had been dairy herds and horses, cats and dogs. There had been my pony Jessa; but she had been an occasional pet, to be ridden in the holidays and left behind when the parents and I returned to Neustadt, our home south of Vienna.

My mother wouldn't allow animals in the house. Her excuse was that they were unhygienic and might infect me with some dreadful disease. She had a fixed idea that I was delicate and had to be kept away from other children and animals. There was little understanding between us. She had wanted a son and I don't think she ever got over the disappointment of giving birth to a daughter. Compensating for her lack of love she subjected me to exaggerated health-care. I was watched and plagued by a succession of doctors and nannies, dressed in too many layers and washed too frequently in antiseptic solutions. Isolated from kids of my own age I retaliated by rejecting all toys and by demanding excessive attention from my father. He and I were deeply fond of one another; he spent every free moment with me, and by the time I was four he had taught me to read and write.

On my fifth birthday he somehow persuaded mother to

let me go to school. She had planned to have me educated by tutors. Instead an English governess was engaged whose first duty was to take me to the co-educational Lutheran school, to fetch me after lessons and to make sure that I did not mix with the other children outside school hours.

No other child had a constant escort. The school, attached to a small church, was in the centre of our small town. There was hardly any traffic and most parents considered the streets safe enough to let their kids go unaccompanied. Of course I hated being made an exception.

One day a wonderful thing happened; a master had gone sick and we were sent home an hour early. For once my governess was not waiting at the gate. I walked out alone into the winter sun feeling happy, guilty and excited.

I was in the streets on my own for the first time and the beauty of our mediaeval town took me by surprise. It seemed as if I'd never before seen the massive wall which had kept out the Turkish invaders of Austria in the 16th century, the monastery built by Leopold Babenberg in the 13th century, or the graceful baroque houses with their golden yellow walls and white window frames. Wandering at leisure over the uneven cobbles I looked at the shop windows which were displaying St Nicholas in his bishop's robes and an assortment of black and red devils — traditional figures of the feast of St Nicholas.

I stood and gazed at the market square with its ancient cloistered covered walks and the stalls in the centre where Hungarian farm-wives from across the border and small-holders from the town were selling everything from live geese and home-made cheese to prunes and vegetables. I'd always disliked having to eat; yet, suddenly I felt hungry. I went up to a policeman and asked him to lend me ten groschen. Of course he did; my father was the Commissioner of Police.

Frau Pokorny, one of our cook's favourite stall holders, sold me a bag of apples and a poke of hot chestnuts and on I went to Wiener Street to look at the windows of Riha, one of the few big stores in the town. Mr Riha always had a good display but that time it was special. His St Nicholas was presiding over clockwork devils who were swarming over mountains of sheets and pillowslips, throwing snowballs at one another. Even more exciting, beside St Nicholas sat a small coffee-coloured dog — a live dog with a long face and floppy ears.

As I gazed at him a boy, about twice my age, came from behind a stack of sheets, picked up the dog and disappeared. Presently he and the dog came out of the store and sat down on the steps under the canopy. The boy was Freddy Kessler, the elder brother of a girl who went to my school.

'Is he your dog?' I asked

'No, it's Mr Riha's new puppy. His name is Gruber.'

'Why is it Gruber?'

'He's called after the new Admira centre half.'

'What's that?'

'A centre half? Don't you know anything about football? Well, I suppose girls don't.'

'May I stroke Gruber?'

'He'll bite you if he doesn't like you.'

Gruber growled when I tried to pick him up but he didn't object to being stroked. After a while he rolled on his back and trustfully presented his chest. Freddy explained that I was lucky; Gruber had accepted me into the small privileged group of people he didn't bite.

We sat playing with Gruber, oblivious of the many legs going up and down the shop stairs, unaware of the changing light until the street lamps went bright.

Even after I'd torn myself away from Gruber and Freddy Kessler I didn't go home immediately. I wandered down the avenue which led past our house to the canal, an attractive waterway which had once linked Neustadt with Vienna. The magic day of freedom had not yet ended; the moonlit water, flanked by snow-covered fields, held me enthralled until the cold became unbearable.

Not until I let myself into our garden did I think of my mother. I crept into the kitchen, was embraced by our huge cook and carried to the drawing room, followed by my weeping governess and several maids. Cook delivered me into my father's arms. I think the whole staff would have given notice if my mother had shown her true feelings.

That night my parents quarrelled. It was the first and last time they clashed. I lay in bed, listening to them hurting one another, feeling more lonely than ever. The worst of it was that I had to stay put; a five-year old just couldn't leave home. There was no escape from the domination of adults. The future, when I'd be free to go exploring the world on my own, seemed hopelessly remote.

Trying to shut out the angry voices I switched on the bedside lamp and began to read my favourite book, Selma Lagerlöf's story of a sleigh-dog. Suddenly the image of the white husky turned into a vision of Gruber. With me was the feel of that warm, silky coat; I saw the dark eyes big with concentration — as if the whole of the dog was intent on discovering all about me.

I was partly awakened by a whispering beside my bed.

'Do you think she heard us?' asked my mother.

'No. Don't worry darling,' my father comforted her.

'I must have been mad to make a scene outside her door . . . or make a scene at all.'

'I am sorry too. I didn't mean what I said.'

'Then you should have meant it Richard. I've been very stupid about Madelaine.'

Father gently took the book out of my hands. 'She's been reading her dog story again. How about letting her have a puppy for Christmas?'

'No, please. Not a dog.'

CHAPTER TWO

No dog. But my father had won a victory. Never again was I escorted to school by an adult, never again did I have to suffer the humiliation of being the only child to be taken home by a governess.

Between home and school I was allowed to explore our ancient town and to visit the places where my fellow pupils lived. I came to know the spicey smell of leather at the shoemakers, the jewel-coloured jars at the chemists, the feel of sawdust at the carpenters, the sounds of the knitting machine at the woolshop.

But what I liked best was to see craftsmen at work. Herr Frankel, the wraithlike Jewish silversmith, encouraged his daughter Rebecca to invite her friends. While Frau Frankel fed us home-made honey cake, he'd demonstrate the making of jewellery and silver cups. The sense of excitement I felt when a hot flame turned the grey metal to translucent sunset pink is something that grips me even now, when I make silver objects in my own workshop.

Herr Kessler, father of Emma and Freddy, was another craftsman who influenced me for life. In his workshops began my interest in minerals, from common sandstone to the most precious. Though he was chiefly a builder his favourite part of the business was the carving of memorials and grave stones. He often used me and his own children as models for cherubs and it was fun to see our images sprout wings.

Though I was made welcome in many homes and places of work I somehow remained an outsider. The isolation of the first five years of my life had made me extremely shy and reserved. My fellow pupils and their parents liked me but they didn't quite know what to make of so silent a child. My only close friends were Gruber, the dachshund, and Freddy.

With the consent of Gruber's bearded owner Freddy and

I took the dog for long walks in the park of the Military Academy or along the canal. I don't know why Freddy, at the age of twelve, became the companion of a six year old but I do know why I became so attached to him. I liked his thin face with the pleasing bone structure, the clear dark eyes with their fast-changing expressions and the quiet voice which told me something new every time we met.

It was Freddy who bridged the gap in our ages in an astonishingly short time. In the beginning he taught me how to identify breeds of cats and dogs, told me the names of flowers and trees and explained natural phenomena such as rainbows and Halley's comet. By the time I was ten and he sixteen we were sharing an enthusiasm for Plato's *Republic* and the political writings of Machiavelli. But the book that sparked off my abiding interest in politics in relation to communities and individuals was Arnold Zweig's novel *The Case of Sergeant Grischa.* No book had ever moved me more deeply and I still possess the copy which Freddy gave me on my twelfth birthday.

Intellectual curiosity was only one side of Freddy's personality. He was also an outstanding athlete and a craftsman. He was a strong swimmer and a fine skater. Eventually I could keep up with him in the water and partner him on the icerink, but when he played football Gruber and I just sat and watched his team. It was enough for me to know the rules and to be able to discuss the games. On Sundays he often worked on a sculpture for his father. Rejecting the sentimental cherubs and weeping women so many townspeople liked to put on family graves, he carved patterns of branches and animals which were much more artistic but didn't sell nearly so well. For me he made a good luck charm, a funny little chimney-sweep carved in ivory.

I suppose Freddy was a genius, and because he was so talented the boys of his own age treated him as a vaguely respected outsider. Looking back, it seems natural that Freddy played Pygmalion, created companions of his choice, and became Gruber's friend and mine.

Freddy rarely entered our house because he sensed that

my mother disliked our association. My father on the other hand became very fond of him and made the two of us welcome at his offices. Police Headquarters was a 14th century town house with superb vaulted ceilings. On grey, snow-laden winter afternoons we'd often sit beside father's ornate wood-burning china stove, eat apples from the roasting-tray and talk about Tolstoy and the poverty of Austria's workers, about football and why the Nazi party was outlawed in Austria.

My father, as a qualified international lawyer and Commissioner of Police, had a professional interest in politics. He was frequently consulted by the Government of the day. A boyhood friend of Prince Starhemberg and Dr Dollfuss, the Chancellor of Austria, he was sent on government missions abroad. On several occasions he'd met Mussolini and Hitler.

In common with most of his contemporaries father believed that Mussolini was good for Italy (because he made the trains run on time), and that Hitler and his Nazi party were doomed to an early failure. As a young man he'd witnessed the Hungarian revolution of Bela Kun, he'd seen the right wing *enemies* strung up on Budapest's lamp posts, and he was convinced that Communism was a much greater evil than Nazism.

Freddy, politely and firmly, disagreed. I can still see him perched on the edge of father's desk, dark eyes troubled, foretelling an age of violence and the end of our world. I felt no fear. I was still a child. What did politics matter compared to Gruber? Gruber lying on his back, a foxy smile on his face, firelight turning his coat the colour of early chestnuts; Gruber dancing on his hind legs in pursuit of an apple; Gruber curled into a little ball, head tucked beneath his feathery tail.

Gruber and I were alone when the shooting started. Freddy had gone skiing with his school. Mother, extremely worried for reasons I didn't yet understand, appeared to be unaware of my existence. Cook and the rest of the staff, looking serious, kept themselves to themselves. And my father hadn't been seen for twenty-four hours.

On our usual walk Gruber behaved oddly. He ignored the dogs he'd normally greet or growl at, he refrained from chasing the squirrels in the park and he stayed close beside me all the way. When we got back to Riha's he slunk inside and crept under a counter. I sat down beside him, asking what was the matter, stroking the shivering little body. Gruber's nose was reassuringly cold, but something was upsetting him.

Gradually I became aware that the store was empty except for the sales girls who stood around talking quietly. And I realized that the distant noise we'd been hearing was gunfire. There were other uncommon sounds; of crowds fast-marching over the cobbles and of angry, raucous voices.

Herr Riha came out of his office and gave orders to close the store. I went and took him to Gruber's hiding place, telling him that something was wrong with the dog.

He picked up his dachs. 'He's scared,' he told me. 'And we've got something to be scared about. You should be at home, Madelaine. Don't you know? there are riots in town. And there's fighting on the outskirts; the unemployed have been trying to blow up the locomotive factory.'

'Why?'

'Because they're hungry. They're sick of the hardships they've suffered for so many years. The Government's broken a promise to give them work. Now they want to get rid of the Government.'

'There won't be work for them if they blow up factories.'

'That's right Madelaine. It's what your father is trying to tell them. You'd better stay with us. I'll phone your mother and tell her that you're safe.'

That night I slept in the apartment above the store with Gruber on the pillow beside me.

By morning the town was silent again and Herr Riha drove me home. And still no one paid attention to me. My father had returned by ambulance and there were two doctors at his bedside. He had been injured in the riot at the factory; there was a danger that he'd lose the sight of his right eye.

Weeks later, when he had fully recovered, one of his men at Police Headquarters told me what had happened. Father had faced a great mob of rioters, some of them armed. He'd refused to let his policemen and gendarmes use their guns. He'd stood his ground at the factory gates, pleading with the mob, promising to make the Government deal immediately with the terrible problems of unemployment. He had almost calmed the rioters when a few men in the crowd began to throw stones at him. He was hit on the head and knocked unconscious. When the people saw him lie bleeding on the ground they turned away and quietly went home. It was the end of the revolution in Wiener Neustadt, the beginning of an uneasy, shortlived peace.

In winter Freddy and I usually took Gruber to the Military Academy's park, close to the town centre, where the avenues were kept clear of snow. When the days lengthened we preferred the countryside. We'd walk along the canal until it veered north-west towards Vienna and then take a path which led south through fields of sweet corn to a patch of no-man's land. Crossing a copse of willow trees and a meadow we'd get to the River Leitha.

At that point the river was the frontier between Austria and Hungary.

That's where we went on the first hot day of 1934. We'd taken swim suits but the water — melted snow from the Rax mountains — was still icy. We gave up the idea of swimming and lay down in the sun. There was a scent of clover and wild violets. We read. We talked. We played with Gruber, who was convinced that humans stretched on the ground solely for his benefit so that he could walk all over them, leap from one to the other, nuzzle their ears and ruffle hair.

Suddenly Gruber quivered, stood up, head cocked, tail high, and streaked off. For a small dog he had a big bark, and he was making a lot of noise. We'd never met anyone

A perfect Portrait of Gruber by Miss Mercy Creed

in this quiet spot of ours; now about a dozen young men came climbing up the river bank. They formed a single file and went marching off towards the town. They had parcels strapped to their backs, long, heavy-looking packages wrapped in sacking.

Gruber, still barking, was racing beside the column when the leader lashed out with his jackboot and sent him sprawling. Gruber yelped with pain, but he picked himself up and went limping back to us.

'Damned bastards!'

It was the only time I'd heard Freddy swear. I picked up the dog and held him while Freddy gently examined him.

'Nothing broken,' he assured me. 'But that thug Wolf certainly bruised Gruber's hip.'

'You know the man who did it?'

'We both know him. Don't you remember? He used to be a neighbour of yours.'

'Wolf Mokkri? I wouldn't have recognized him. He wasn't all that big when he went to boarding school.'

'Some boarding school! The Hitler Youth in Germany.

Wolf's father shipped a lot of boys to Munich. He's something important in the Nazi Party.'

'But there isn't a Nazi Party in Austria.'

'Oh yes, there is. Making it illegal hasn't finished it off. On the contrary; the illegals are heroes now. You know what these boys were carrying? Guns. They were smuggling guns from Hungary.'

'How do you know Freddy?'

'The shape of the packages. Besides, they've been around our place. They want father and me to join the Party. They said it would be bad for our business if we don't.'

'They can't do anything to you.'

'They've got the guns.'

'My father's men have got guns too.'

'Look; your father's men are trying to catch the Nazi smugglers. They're successful some of the time. But the Nazis also succeed some of the time. The difference that counts between them and your father's policemen is that the police won't use their guns, but the Nazis will.'

'They're not gangsters,' I argued. 'They're our own people. You went to school with them . . .'

'They left my school when we were fifteen, and went to Germany. They've changed. Something's been done to them. You'll see. They will use those guns.'

While my mother and I were at my grandparents' estate, playing tennis and riding, the Nazis Planetta and Holzweber did use their guns. They struck on 24th July 1934.

Confused radio bulletins informed us that there had been a coup d'etat in Vienna, that the Government had been deposed, that Chancellor Dollfuss had been badly wounded in the shooting, that the Nazis had taken over the country, that Dollfuss had fled, that fighting had broken out.

My mother was desperately worried about father, who had stayed at his post, and decided to return with me to Wiener Neustadt. She had difficulties in hiring a car. It was evening before we set out towards Vienna.

The capital was an extraordinary sight. There were candles burning in every window, thousands upon thousands of candles, in every house, in every street and square. The city, looking like a vast funeral pyre, seemed deserted.

We stopped at Police Headquarters and found an inspector. Yes, he told us, my father had been in Vienna all day but he'd returned to Wiener Neustadt. What was happening?

'The Nazi revolt is over,' he said. 'Dr Dollfuss has died. . . They gunned him down, but he wasn't dead when they carried him into the Chancellery. He might have been saved if those Nazi criminals had let him have medical help. But they wouldn't let a doctor in. He bled to death . . . They let him bleed to death. We'll crucify the Nazi murderers.'

In Neustadt the only obvious effect of the abortive Nazi rising was that the Jewish community made itself as inconspicuous as possible. On warm summer evenings the main roads of the town and the market square had always been the meeting place of the young people. They strolled around or frequented the tables outside coffee house, exchanging news, planning the future and falling in love. The Jewish young had been a natural part of the scene. Suddenly they were missing. And on Friday night the Jews did not, as usual, linger outside the synagogue; they went home by the shortest route.

Freddy told me that several Jews had been attacked on the day of the Chancellor's assassination. Our friend, the silversmith Frankel, had suffered worst. Nazi thugs had broken into his shop and beaten him up. He was in hospital with fractured ribs.

We went to visit Herr Frankel. His body, covered with a sheet, looked very small and frail. He was pleased to see us and yet embarrassed. He kept apologising for his appearance, saying he wasn't fit to be seen by decent people. His face was disfigured with cuts and bruises; the eyes were swollen and bloodshot, the hair had been crudely cut off where they'd had to stitch his scalp.

'The nurse said he'd be well quite soon,' I consoled Freddy as we were leaving the ward.

Freddy remained silent. He seemed terribly shocked, so much so that he was unable to hide his distress.

Under the chestnut trees in the hospital garden be abruptly stopped and faced me. 'Madelaine, you must go away. Leave Austria. The sooner the better. Go to England.'

'But that's silly. I don't . . .'

'Listen to me!' He was close to tears. 'You must go. Your father was educated in England, wasn't he? He's got friends. Tell him you want to go to an English school. Do you hear? Insist on it. You always get what you want when you really try.You must try hard . . . No, don't argue. Promise me you'll do it.'

I promised. I think I'd have promised anything to make Freddy feel less upset.

Third from left (front) my father, fourth (front) Dr. Dollfuss, Chancellor of Austria, shortly before his assassination. Behind Dr. Dollfuss (right) Prince Starhemberg.

Though Freddy never referred to Herr Frankel's experience of violence he did mention something which showed that he was preoccupied with the attack on our Jewish friend.

He said, 'Next time it might be me.'

I misunderstood. I thought he was scared of getting beaten up. 'But you're not a Jew, Freddy.'

'Don't you see? The Nazis aren't giving up. They keep trying to make me join their Party.'

Mother refused to resume the holiday on my grandparents' estate. She wouldn't leave Neustadt without father. And my father, who had been transferred to Headquarters in Vienna, wouldn't take a rest until Dr Schuschnigg had formed a new government and the political situation was under control.

The conflagration of candles on the night of Dr Dollfuss's death had been a gesture of bowing to authority rather than an expression of mourning. The country did seem calmer.

Money had been pumped into the run-down Neustadt industries and the unemployment figures were going down — which kept the Socialists content for the moment. And the impending trial of Dr Dollfuss's assassins kept the Nazis quiet.

Freddy, Gruber and I were joined by a new friend who did much to convince me that life was fun and there was nothing to worry about. I suspect that Hans Phillip attached himself to us because he wanted to make drawings of Gruber.

Hans had been kicked out of every school in Neustadt because he was totally resistant to discipline. Eventually his parents had found a tough school in Vienna which somehow succeeded in making him pass matriculation. At last Hans had come to the point he'd wanted to reach ever since his early childhood; his parents agreed to let him study art. Hans had no ambitions, no interests, beyond drawing, painting and girls. His favourite girl was Freddy's sister, Emma.

Hans owned a beat-up motorbicycle with a side-car.

He'd collect us early in the morning and take us to Fischau, a little village near Neustadt with two crystal-clear thermal swimming pools at the edge of magnificent pine forests.

'Have you heard this one,' he'd shout above the roar of the motorbike. *This one* would always be a comical story. '. . . So the Pope invited the priests to dinner . . . every cleric who'd applied for the new envoyship. In the middle of the banquet . . . they eat fantastically well at the Vatican . . . a very rude and unplanned sound escaped from the Holy Father. The English priest blushed and said *Sorry. Granted,* said the Pope. After a while it happened again . . . that shocking sound. The French priest bowed and said, *I beg your pardon, Your Holiness. You are forgiven,* said the Pope. And then, just when there was a very reverend silence because the brandy was so great, the Pope emitted the rude sound yet again. . . Do you know why the American cleric didn't get the new envoy job? . . . No? Well, I'll tell you. You see, the American sort of sniffed and said, *Not to worry; have this one on me Your Holiness.'*

Hans had an unending supply of such stories. We hadn't chosen his company, yet we soon missed him when he wasn't around. Even Gruber, who didn't care for new people, did his best for Hans by posing for numerous sketches. For Gruber to keep still as much as five minutes at a time was an act of love.

It was a wonderful summer, and I had no desire to leave my friends. But towards the end of August father was at last able to take a holiday and we went to Italy for a couple of weeks. I was happy in Venice, yet I looked forward to our homecoming.

On the morning after our return Hans and Gruber called. Both of them seemed more subdued than usual. For once Hans was not bursting with funny stories. He was polite to my parents. He had a cup of coffee with us in the garden, but he was obviously relieved when my parents went indoors.

'Let's go to the Kesslers,' he said, as soon as we were

alone. 'I want to be with Emma. . . She's terribly worried about Freddy. He's left home . . . Just went away three days ago. No one knows why. No one knows where he is.'

'It isn't like Freddy,' said Frau Kessler. Hans, Emma and I were sitting in her kitchen, helping her peel apples for a pie. 'He's always told us where he was going. And he never went far, did he? Just to the mountains . . . I remember the time his school went to France. Not Freddy. He said he didn't want to go abroad; if he wanted to know about foreign places he could read about them. . . He said only the other day that he couldn't live anywhere but in Austria . . . It was a funny thing for him to say; it isn't as if we'd ever expected him to go away.'

I said, 'He wants me to go to a school in England.'

'That's different. Your parents have friends and relations in other countries. You're not really Neustadters . . . Maybe Freddy's right; with the Nazis in power you'd be safer abroad.'

'You think the Nazis will take over, Frau Kessler?'

'Yes.' Through the open door, she watched Gruber sniff his way across the builders' yard to the orchard. 'God help us.'

Gruber went tracking on under the iron gate, the tip of his feathery tail quivering above daisies and buttercups.

'It'll be a sick dachshund tonight,' said Hans. 'He's sure to eat too many apples.'

Very likely. Gruber knew no restraint when it came to fruit.

Emma smiled. 'At least the apples are ripe.'

I got up to fetch Gruber. Freddy certainly wouldn't allow the dog to give himself a bellyache.

There was a Sunday emptiness in the yard. A half-loaded lorry was standing by the workshops, terracotta bricks glowing in the sun. As the deep boom of the dome-bells and the tinkle from the monastery church stopped, the orchard became so quiet that I could hear the whispering of the grasses in Gruber's wake.

Suddenly Gruber made a sound that made me shiver. I'd never before heard him emit that awful, long-drawn howl.

With visions of Gruber attacked by a snake or Gruber caught in a rat trap I rushed to the bottom of the orchard. Gruber's howling had changed to a whining that sounded human.

I found the dog in a thicket of red currant bushes, at Freddy's feet. Freddy was lying on his back, wide open eyes staring into the sky. There was a smile on his lips, the familiar expression of welcome, yet I knew that he was dead.

Knowing how Gruber hated being picked up, I lay down beside the miserably crying dog and took his head in my hands. That's what had comforted him when he'd had a toothache. It wasn't helping this time. Gruber was crying with all of his small body.

I couldn't cry. I could only see with a terrible clarity why Freddy had killed himself. He'd been too afraid to go on living, scared that one day the thugs who had hurt Herr Frankel would become so powerful that they'd force him into committing brutalities. And so Freddy had made his choice.

I lay there, sick with pain, thinking of what had happened to *me,* feeling sorry for myself. All at once the dog stopped crying; he was having trouble with his breathing, gasping for air.

I gathered him into my arms and began to massage his chest and throat. 'Quiet,' I pleaded. 'It's all over now. You'll be all right Gruber, please . . .' Having to watch the suffering of so small a creature was unbearable.

It was anxiety for Gruber, not self-pity, which made me weep. And then I felt the little body relax. Gruber gave a deep sigh, put out his tongue and began to lick the tears off my face.

What Freddy had foreseen as early as 1934 happened; the Nazi take-over in Austria, the deaths of millions in concentration camps and in the war, the end of all the things which had made up our world and Gruber's.

I kept my promise to Freddy and went to England. As the train steamed out of the Vienna railway station, as the white handkerchiefs fluttered above the sad faces of my parents, of Hans Phillip and many other friends from Neustadt, I sensed that the separation was final.

My parents were killed at Minsk concentration camp. Hans, the exuberant, clowning artist did what Freddy would have been too gentle to do. He fought a war of his own. Neustadt became the only town in Austria where a highly effective resistance movement opposed Nazism throughout the war. Hans, a leader of the resistance, died while blowing up a munition train.

As the Russian troops advanced on Neustadt I received a Red Cross message from Herr Riha. *Gruber died of old age, peacefully in his sleep.*

CHAPTER THREE

Normally I don't dwell on the past, because all I can do for the dead is to live for the living. But when it comes to inviting a new person or animal into our family I want to understand my motives as much as Alex does. And motives — as I've learned in medicine and as a writer — are often rooted in a past as submerged as Atlantis. I am convinced of one thing; that one shouldn't use the people or animals one lives with as emotional lightning-conductors.

Of course one doesn't always have a choice whether or not to admit a creature into one's home. There are those who just turn up and won't go away, such as the butterfly and the ladybird who took over our first home in Brighton.

I found Sylvie, the butterfly, one cold November morning in the spare room. When she was still there the day after I took it that she wanted to winter with us and began to worry about her diet. I telephoned a number of friends, from vets to farmers. The consensus of advice was that Sylvie should be kept supplied with saucers of honey-water.

The problem of Sylvie was obviously settled to her satisfaction when Roger showed up. It was Kathy, our home-help, who christened the ladybird. Roger he was because he'd emerged from the pages of Roget's Thesaurus. From the book he flew to my typewriter, where he settled on one of the ribbon-spools. I didn't notice him on the dangerous machine until I saw him spin like a child on a round-about. For days after I dared not use the typewriter for fear of getting Roger trapped in the works. But Roger, by sheer persistence, let me know that he too had come to stay and that he considered the ribbon-spool roundabout an amenity of the home.

This time vets, farmers and doctors were not so sure how I could help our unusual guest to survive. Some suggested small drops of honey-water, others flowers or house-plants infested with greenfly.

Unable to find infested houseplants, I had to serve Roger clean ones and honey-water. I never saw him feed, but a couple of weeks later he was still emerging from Roget's Thesaurus, flying to the typewriter or taking a stroll on the curtains in front of my desk.

At Christmas, wanting to give Roger a treat, I brought him a bunch of mimosa. I carefully set him down on a fragrant, fluffy bloom, picked up a magnifiying glass and prepared to observe his joy. In no time at all Roger showed unmistakable displeasure. As if I'd set him down in a quagmire his legs began to lift and kick. After a while, still heavy with yellow pollen, he extricated himself and flew back to his favourite book. Safely landed, he began to dust himself down, cleaning leg against leg, working away irritably until every particle of mimosa was stripped off and lying on the printed page.

While Sylvie was either fluttering around the apartment, showing off the peacock colours of her wings, or visibly asleep on the bedcover, Roger presented a major problem. Though he was a creature of habit, usually occupying the same spots, he did occasionally stray. Kathy and I never dared to use the vacuum cleaner or a duster until we'd established Roger's whereabouts. Only then, while one of us kept a watch on the ladybird, did the other get on with the cleaning. By the spring Alex, Kathy and I were fully butterfly and ladybird-trained.

None of us saw Sylvie leave her winter quarters. She just disappeared. But Roger made an exit befitting his sense of drama. One sunny morning, when the trees in the square had unfolded their young golden-green leaves, Roger took an extra long spin on my typewriter ribbon. From there he landed on my hand, walked up and down like a fashion model displaying the new season's clothes, flexed his wings and took off into the spring.

It had been a long journey from Gruber to Sylvie and Roger, from Neustadt to Brighton. In Neustadt people had not, as a rule, gone in for pets. In Sussex, especially when we moved from Brighton to the village across the Downs, most of our neighbours were owned by cats or dogs.

We were in the process of buying the cottage when the estate agent informed us that our future neighbour had telephoned him. Miss Frederica, a lady of the Victorian era, had obviously been brought up to giving instructions to tradesmen and the like.

She had told the agent, 'I understand that you have two clients who wish to purchase the cottage next door. One is a retired police officer from the Colonies, the other a doctor whose wife is an author. Please arrange for the cottage to be sold to the young couple. I wish to remind you that it was the home of author Jefferson Farjeon. I think it would be appropriate for the cottage to remain in literary hands.'

When the sale had gone through I decided to put Miss Frederica's mind at rest and to pay my respects in a manner to which she must have been accustomed in her youth. Leaving cards had become an obsolete custom, but I made a visiting card and handed it to her home-help, Mrs Cox.

Within the hour Miss Frederica telephoned, inviting me to take a glass of sherry with her.

No one answered the front door bell when I called at the appointed time. Hearing strange noises from within Miss Frederica's cottage, I took the overgrown path to the side. The garden was a jungle of tall flowers, shrubs and old fruit trees. On a bird table, festooned with coconuts and strips of fat, bluetits and coaltits were performing delightful acrobatics. On branches all around me thrushes and blackbirds let fly their evening song.

'This year we have a nightingale,' Mrs Cox greeted me. 'We think it lives in the cyprus tree over in your garden . . . This way.' She led me into a sooty little kitchen full of dirty dishes. 'Miss Frederica likes to receive in the dining room. Best fireplace in the house. We like a good coal fire winter and summer, on account of the rheumatism.' Mrs Cox's round little body certainly showed signs of rheumatism, but she had a beautiful Romany face and the heavy hair — arranged like a coronet — was still jet black. 'Ma'am,' she opened a much-scratched brown door, 'Here's your neighbour that will be.'

The old lady who stood up to meet me was very tall and heavy. She too had a handsome face, but of the Anglo-Saxon blue-eyed type. 'My dear, how charming of you to call.' Her smile was warm and full of fun. 'You must forgive my Mrs Cox, but she just won't answer the front door. But, of course, she's a remarkable woman. You know she was a model for Frank Brangwyn, the painter, who used to live in our village. He was very famous. He even painted murals in the Rockefeller Center in New York.' While she was talking she was sweeping piles of newspapers from a chair by the fire, straightening a dirty, dog-eared rug and shifting a vase of dead flowers from the dining table to a Welsh dresser. The smell of dust and neglect was overpowering.

'Yes, Mrs Cox is quite remarkable,' Miss Frederica waved me to the cleared chair, 'But not, I may say, as a domestic help. I'm not sure which of us two is the worse housekeeper. My excuse is that I never lived alone until recently . . .'

Miss Frederica gave me a short, unsentimental account of her life. Brought up on a large estate run by a staff of servants. Death of her fiance in the First World War. Death of father. Death duties. Gradual impoverishment. Move to a large flat in Brighton, with mother and the last couple of servants. Recent death of mother.

'But I still have my animals,' she told me cheerfully, 'Tiger! Mufoo! where are you? Come and be introduced.'

The door opposite the kitchen opened wider and in crept a very ancient pekingese and a large siamese cat. Tiger, the dog, sniffed at my legs in a perfunctory way, gave a growl that ended in a weary grunt, and flopped down in front of the fire. Mufoo, who was blind, sharpened her claws on my chair, felt her way to the arm, and gave a mighty leap — landing on my shoulder.

'Mufoo, kindly go down at once,' commanded Miss

Frederica. 'You know perfectly well that you mustn't be a nuisance when someone calls for the first time.'

The siamese, looking distinctly sulky, descended my arm, puncturing my skin on the way.

'I see you're a dog-person,' said Miss Frederica. 'So am I. It's a little like being right-handed or left-handed. One either favours dogs or cats. But there's one important difference. In my experience cat-persons are usually so single-minded about their pets that they deprive themselves of the companionship of dogs. Among dog-persons, on the other hand, there are those who are — so to speak — ambidexterous. Capable of appreciating cats almost as much as dogs. What are you my dear?'

'I am probably ambidexterous. But I have no experience of cats.'

'Never mind. Mufoo will certainly train you. I believe she's too old to catch birds, but one never knows. Keep an eye on her when she visits your garden . . . I originally acquired Mufoo for keeping down the mice. But I should have known better. Siamese are far too superior to trouble themselves with vermin; though I do think that Mufoo has scared away my deathwatch beatle if not the ordinary woodworm. . . My dear, I quite forgot. The sherry, Mrs Cox!'

Mrs Cox limped in, carrying a tarnished silver tray with two little glasses. 'We're out of sherry ma'am, so I've brought the Jamikey.'

'Jamaica rum, Mrs Cox, Jamaica rum. I'm sure our future neighbour won't mind.' She lifted her glass, bright blue eyes laughing. 'Down the hatch . . . I do hope you like rum. It's the speciality of this house. We always had at least one sailor in the family. My dear mother used to say *an admiral in the family*. She was a wonderful lady but — between you and me — something of a snob. I expect it was a little matter of background. She didn't come from a landed family like my father's; her people were in coal . . . Now my dear, tell me. When will you take up residence next door?'

'At the end of the month.'

'That will be nice . . . I do think Lewis has been clever about modernizing your cottage. Of course, you know, he is the Alliance Building Society, so he must have experience.'

Lewis Cohen, the former owner of the cottage, had wisely installed a modern bathroom and vastly enlarged the kitchen before putting the place on the market. But he'd covered up the cracks with so many different wall papers that it finished up as a psychedelic nightmare.

'I did think the walls were a little too exuberant,' said Miss Frederica, 'and I'm thankful that you're changing the decor . . . I'm sure you don't mind; I've been inspecting your new home from time to time. Now. When you've taken up residence I'll give a cocktail party so that you can meet your new neighbours properly. Yes, I've quite made up my mind; a Sunday noon party. I'll invite a bishop or two. It's always wise to have a bishop when you have drinks immediately after church on Sunday . . . Now; who else should be invited. Let me see . . .'

I hadn't intended to stay until nightfall, but there was no getting away from Miss Frederica's thumbnail sketches of our future neighbours. There was Wendy-and-Martin; related to Anthony Eden; he was a lawyer; they had a boy and a girl; all extremely nice. There was Rowland-and-Mary; Rowland Emmet, who invented that funny railway and contributed those wonderful cartoons in Punch. There were the McIntoshes, who grew alpine flowers and believed in spiritualism; and Miss Joy, who had at least ten dachshunds; and Miss Rawlins, who was a fine painter.

'But I won't invite the screamers,' declared Miss Frederica. 'I know it's naughty of me and they'll be cross with me, but I won't have them. Not in your party. . . I call them the screamers, father, mother, and son, because you can hear their rather exaggerated Oxford accents all through the lane. The screamers are quite nice, of course; just a little arrogant and selfish. There are others like them in this village. You mustn't mind them, my dear. I believe you come from the Continent; well — between you and me — people like the screamers are rather parochial and narrow minded. Face them with someone from abroad and they'll be quite suspicious . . . that the stranger isn't top drawer. Needless to say, it's only people who themselves aren't top-drawer who worry about such minor details. You'll certainly be made welcome by the village and the *real* county people.'

Shortly before nine o'clock I noticed Miss Frederica glance at her television and realized that she was willing to let me go. She accompanied me to the front door.

'On the day you move in,' she said, 'you and the removal men must come for tea at any time.'

Suddenly the quiet lane filled with voices. 'Dawling . . . dawling where are you? I say, old girl, what have you done with my deah stalker? I can't find it anywhere!'

'But dawling, it must be in the hall.'

'Dawling, it isn't. Do you think the puppy's eaten it?'

'Oh! you don't really need the deah stalker.'

'But dawling, I do. I want to fetch a bottle from the cellar. Dawling . . .'

Miss Frederica laughed. 'There. Now you know all about the screamers. But don't worry, they go to bed early . . . It'll be lovely having you next door, my dear . . . By the way, do you have a feeling for beef?'

I discovered the answer to that mysterious question a few days after we'd moved into the cottage.

Miss Frederica's head appeared above the hedge. 'Is Mufoo being a nuisance?' she asked.

'Oh no, not at all.' Mufoo, clambering about my kitchen, had just made me stow away my shopping in a great rush. Nothing even remotely edible was safe from those powerful jaws.

'Good.' Miss Frederica sounded absent minded. 'Mr Andrews has just delivered a very good-looking joint. I'm having a dinner party tonight. . .Madelaine, I'd very much value your opinion of the beef. I believe there are various methods of cooking joints. Our cook used to say it's a matter of feeling. If you could look in this afternoon, just for a minute . . .'

I went to my study on the first floor and continued work on the current book until papa-screamer's voice trumpeted me back into the here and now.

'Dawling, where are you? Dawling I've made a perfectly gorgeous cuppa!'

Four o'clock. Cat-time. Mufoo and I had come to a gentleman's agreement; she would not sneak in, leap upon me and puncture my skin at any time provided I went to the kitchen at four and served her a bowl of milk.

Mufoo had a highly accurate built-in clock. She was waiting for me.

'Dawling,' called the screamer, 'Do come and drink your cuppa. It's Dawjeeling from Fornum's!'

'Be with you in a jiffy,' answered mamma-screamer. 'Oh, I say! what a ghastly lot of smoke! Do you think Miss Frederica's set herself on fire?'

'Good Lord!'

'Dawling, don't you think we should do something?'

'No dawling, positively not. It might be dangerous.'

I shot into the garden, out of our gate, into Miss Frederica's jungle. At the open kitchen door I was almost overwhelmed by acrid fumes.

Miss Frederica, hovering near the cooker, welcomed me with a happy smile. 'Madelaine, how nice. I think you're just in time to give me your opinion of the beef. I put it in at two o'clock . . . I want it to be really nice and tender. Do you think it's safe to open the oven?'

'It would be wise.' I put on the padded glove. 'Stand well back Miss Frederica.'

Having turned off the gas, I opened the oven-door and spun sideways. A tongue of flames leaped forward and dissolved in black smoke. Lesser flames were licking the interior of the oven, burning off thick layers of stale fat.

'Oh dear,' spluttered Miss Frederica, 'I do hope my Yorkshire puddings are all right.'

'We can't look now,' I spluttered back. 'We'll have to leave it for a bit.'

'Never mind. My guests won't be arriving before seven. Come on, I'll show you something.'

She led me into the front hall and stopped before a thick roll of a hideously striped stair carpet. 'Almost new,' she told me, 'such a bargain. You see, my old stair carpet is in holes. I was getting quite worried that Tiger or Mufoo might trip and fall; they're not as young as they were. I've quite made up my mind; tomorrow I'll nail on the new carpet.'

'How will you do it?' I was suspecting the worst.

'Oh, just on top of the old one . . . I'm really quite good with a hammer.'

'Wouldn't you rather have the carpet fixed with clips?'

'Clips? Ah yes, I believe that's the professional way . . . But I fear that would be too complicated for me. Of course, I could try . . .'

I had visions of the old lady lying at the bottom of those steep stairs, with a fractured pelvis or dying of a heart attack. Mrs Cox had told me that she had a dicky heart. 'Let my husband do the carpet for you, Miss Frederica.'

'My dear! A busy doctor! Certainly not. I wouldn't dream of it.'

'But my husband loves doing jobs like this. It's so relaxing . . . it's so good for him.'

'Well, in that case, I accept gratefully. Now. Shall we examine the dinner?'

Of course the joint was as hard and black as a cannon ball and the Yorkshire puddings had turned into a sooty coating on the baking tin.

Miss Frederica, contemplating the disaster, looked slightly worried. 'What a nuisance! It doesn't look at all as I'd intended . . . Perhaps if I boiled the beef . . .'

I shook my head.

'You mean I've ruined it. Oh dear! It's Wednesday and the shops are closed. What am I going to do?' She blew her nose, trying to hide her tears. 'The table is all ready. Look.' She opened the dining room door. She had tidied up and put on an immaculate lace cloth. The table was laid with shining cutlery, silver candlesticks and individual posies of flowers. 'My guests used to be my mother's friends . . . They were coming here for the first time . . . I should telephone and say that I'm unwell . . . Oh dear, I arranged for their chauffeurs to eat at the Bull . . .'

'No, you mustn't cancel the party.'

'Lady John wouldn't have thought much of my cooking even at its best. When she lived in France . . .'

'Miss Frederica, please leave this to me. I'm going to make the dinner. Go upstairs. Rest. Change. And don't come down until five to seven.'

'But we have no meat.'

'Please.'

'Very well, Madelaine. After all, I used to say to my mother that there are times when the young know best.' At the foot of the stairs she had second thoughts. 'Are you sure we can't . . . dress up the joint?'

'Quite sure.'

'I so dislike wasting good food.'

'Perhaps Tiger and Mufoo . . .'

'Feed my dog and my cat on such rubbish! certainly not.'

At six thirty, when Alex came into the study, I was typing the last of the gold-rimmed menu cards.

'*Roulade au vin blanc*,' he read over my shoulder. 'What's that?'

'Bully beef, onions, parsley and spices baked in a sort of pancake, etcetera.'

'And *ivresse de gentilhomme* . . . drunkenness of gentlemen?'

'The pudding.'

'What are you playing at?' he'd taken in my black dress and white frilly apron.

'I'm giving Miss Frederica a hand. No time to explain. Come on, help me carry the dishes next door . . . We'll load everything on the trolley.'

As we made our way through the garden I told Alex about the stair carpet.

'Why doesn't she get a firm to do it?'

'Maybe it didn't occur to her or she can't afford it.'

'Or both,' muttered Alex. 'Bit grim asking me . . .'

'She didn't. I told her you have a passion for carpeting stairs.'

'Thank you Madelaine.'

'It's got to be done tomorrow.'

'Rush job!'

'Yes dawling . . . Oh, and there's no dinner for you. Would you go and get yourself some fish and chips?'

After the party, which Miss Frederica had given for us, she'd joined us for lunch and told us something of the village societies, from the practical to the absurd. There were dozens of them. Miss Frederica had summed up the whole spectrum in her own inimitable way.

'There must be something a little wrong with a community which consists of almost as many committees as families. We are well manicured but I do believe we are a village without a heart. Perhaps it's because the *real* people have gone — the craftsmen and farm workers. The few we have left now live in the council houses outside the village. Their old cottages have been made rather precious and sold to persons who are absorbed in climbing financial or social ladders. They play at being a community. I suspect that they have no real feeling for their neighbours or for country life.'

I had argued that the larger, newer houses and cottages, such as ours, had not been occupied by craftsmen and farm-workers.

'No,' she'd agreed. 'They used to belong to working artists like you; certainly not to the arty-crafty stockbrokers and company directors . . . I don't mean to be uncharitable. One must accept one's fellow men as they are. I just feel a little sad when I think how much genuine professional people like you and Alex contribute to our village and how little they receive in return.'

In time I discovered how truly Miss Frederica had assessed the village. Though I met most of the inhabitants in the shops or at formal cocktail parties, very few ever visited us unless they wanted something. There were little cliques who dropped in at each other's homes, but such cliques remained sealed against ousiders such as us.

Those who did come, uninvited and undemanding, when the spirit moved them, were a delight. Ethel Rawlins, a very old lady and a superb painter of the Sussex landscape, dropped in because she enjoyed talking shop, hers and mine. And Dr Linton-Bogle, Bogey — the village doctor, came to exchange books, play a game of chess, or argue for the pleasure of it. In his spare time — which must have been in the small hours — Bogey practised calligraphy and devised brilliant posters for village festivals.

The most frequent droppers-in of the demanding kind were the screamers, especially papa. He'd retired from commerce at a young age, because he loathed work and had successfully convinced himself that he was in delicate health. Even before we'd moved to the village he'd told Bogey how useful it was going to be to have a doctor on his doorstep. From the beginning he made full use of us both.

Having discovered that I felt sorry for him, he'd walk into our garden and trumpet until I'd invite him in. As his house overlooked the lane he always knew whether or not I was at home. He'd come around six p.m., mix martinis for himself and me downstairs and bring them up to my study like a good host.

'Here we are.' He'd put the drink on my desk and sit himself down on the Victorian couch beside me. 'I say, deah gel,' his pale eyes would take in the typewriter and the stacks of paper. 'You aren't working, are you? Doing all this is frightfully bad for you. . . Now. Time to stop and have your drinkie. . .'

Miss Frederica had told me I shouldn't let the screamers steal my time. But . . . well . . . never having been bored myself, I reckoned that boredom was an affliction and that I couldn't just ignore papa-screamer's suffering.

Poor papa. He died a few years later — chiefly of boredom — after which mamma-screamer retired into her own little circle and never again dropped in on us.

The non-community didn't trouble me because the village gave me the things which solitary people like me enjoy best; pleasure in the fine old buildings, the wonderful views of the hills in their ever changing light, small splits in the earth when daffodils and hyacinths were about to open to the spring sun, the sedate welcome from Miss Frederica's pekinese whenever I passed a certain hole in the hedge at a certain time, and the siamese gracefulness of Mufoo reclining on the couch beside my desk.

Our lane had not been made for so much 20th century plumbing. In heavy rain the drains couldn't cope and our gardens became flooded.

After the first summer storm, when two feet of water lapped against our walls, we asked the District Council to do something about it. We received an evasive reply headed *Alleged Flooding.* We sent snapshots of children sailing boats in the road and a letter headed *De facto Flooding.*

'Alleged' flooding

One day, after years of this correspondence, a gang of workmen appeared and drilled open the road surface. As I walked out with my shopping basket the foreman stopped me.

There was a look of awe in his eyes. 'Just you look at

this, miss . . . A work of art, that's what it is. A work of art. Never seen the like. They don't make them like this any more.'

The exposed drain was built of fine quality brick, superbly pointed and arched like a Roman aqueduct.

'Lovely,' said the foreman, lost in admiration.

By the time I returned from the butcher's the hole had been filled in and the gang had departed. Obviously the foreman's appreciation of art had quashed our appeal for more adequate drainage.

Within a week there was another downpour and the floods rose within a millimetre of the cottages' ground level. To prevent the water from sweeping through the rooms I put on a swimsuit and went to work on the drain-grids in the lane. I was soon joined by the screamer, in deerstalker and muffler, wielding a knight-sized sword.

As we were fishing out twigs and leaves and stabbing away at the grid, Miss Frederica opened one of her upstairs windows.

'How very kind of you,' she said. 'I quite expected the floods to put out my fire. But I've quite made up my mind; I shall stay upstairs until all the water is gone. My swimsuit is so old-fashioned, and I never did look my best in wellington boots.'

I saw her, still tidying up her garden path, working much too hard, and called her in for a cup of coffee.

Talking of our imminent trip to Austria, she seemed sad. 'I miss you when you're away Madelaine. And Mufoo is quite put out; I suppose your chairs are softer than mine. Now, if you don't mind I want to discuss something practical. Between you and me, I'm older than I look. I can't live forever. So I've made suitable arrangements. I'd be grateful if you would make sure that my instructions are carried out. However, should you not be in residence the screamers will telephone Lady John and she will see to everything. I've asked my cousin, the bishop, to write my obituary for the Times. You'll find it with my will in the top right-hand drawer of my desk. Please mail it immediately. My solicitors are to send an announcement of my death to the appropriate papers, but I do not wish them to include any mention of my date of birth or my age. Tiger and Mufoo are too old to settle in a new home. I want them to be put to sleep. . . Now, my dear,' she patted my hand, 'you mustn't upset yourself. I'm perfectly happy at the thought of being re-united with the people I loved who departed before me.'

The subject was closed. Miss Frederica savoured her coffee and took her leave. At the gate she stopped. 'I just remembered; there was something I wanted to ask you. Tell me, do you understand that peculiar experiment the Americans have carried out in the universe? They've released millions of nasty little copper pins in space.'

I said I had read of it in the papers.

'So thoughtless,' she said. 'For all we know the things might scratch the spirits of the departed. What is your opinion?'

I admitted that I hadn't given the copper pins much thought.

'Well, I expect God is equal to new-fangled pollution. I've quite made up my mind about those untidy pins . . . I shall pay no attention to them.'

CHAPTER FOUR

The reason for our journey to Vienna was a small boy who had adopted Alex and me before we were married. For me the relationship had begun immediately after his birth, in the middle of the war, when I'd received the last message from my father before his deportation to Minsk concentration camp. Some compassionate person must have taken the note to Switzerland and forwarded it to my school in Scotland.

Father had written, *Your cousin Marianne has given birth to a son. She is not married. I want you to look for the child when you return to Austria, as I know you will, after the war. Young Paul will need a family.*

Marianne herself had been deprived of a family in circumstances I'd never fully understood. Her mother, my father's sister, had married against grandmother's wish. Marianne's father, badly wounded at the end of the First World War, had died when she was a baby; her mother had committed suicide soon after. My parents had wanted to adopt Marianne, but grandmother had insisted on keeping her. She had grown up on the estate, totally ignored by our harsh and imperious grandmother, educated by whichever stable boy or farmhand could find a little time for her. It had almost been as if our grandmother had made the plain, silent girl pay for her mother's disobedience. In turn Marianne had rejected my parents and me, refusing our invitations to Neustadt, resenting our visits to the estate.

I'd understood why my father had written that Marianne's child would need a family. And after the war I did search for him. I found him, a skinny dark-eyed three year old, alone in an ice cold bomb-damaged room in a tenement.

His mother, he told me, was at work. 'You're from England, aren't you,' he stated.

'That's right.'

'I know. You're my cousin Madelaine. And I am your second cousin Paul. Look, this is my book.' He took me by the hand and made me sit down on the bed beside him. 'I can read.' I must have looked incredulous. 'Really, I can,' he asserted. 'I know, I tell a lot of stories; but this one is true. . . Have you got something to read in your bag?'

I found him a theatre programme. His small index finger traced the top line. *'Die Zau-ber-floete, eine Op-er von Wolf-gang A-ma-deus Mo-zart* . . . You see?'

'You're a very clever boy Paul.'

'I know,' he agreed, without a trace of smugness. 'I'll make tea for us . . . I got the tea from a Russian soldier.'

I was about to say that I'd make the tea when he climbed on a chair and expertly lit a small spirit stove. Every action was neat and assured.

'I can't give you anything else,' he said, when the tea was on the table. 'We have nothing to eat.'

'We have.' I produced the bars of chocolate I'd saved from my ration. 'Hope you like it.'

He unwrapped a bar without tearing the paper and contemplated the brown cubes, eyes large and excited. Then, suddenly, he ran out of the room. 'Minka,' I heard him call, 'Minka, come here.'

He returned with a thin little tabby in his arms. 'Look Minka, we've got something to eat.'

I said, 'Cats don't eat chocolate, Paul.'

'You eat anything when you're hungry.' He broke the bar. 'This is for you . . . this for my mother . . . this for Minka . . . this for me.' The cat grabbed her share and disappeared under the bed. Paul chewed his chocolate with increasing wonder. 'It's nice,' he said, at last.

'Of course it is.'

'No, not of course. We got chocolate from a German soldier once. And it wasn't nice at all. It made me sick.'

When Marianne came in Paul quietly withdrew to the bed and picked up his book. My cousin and I hadn't met since our childhood, yet nothing seemed to have changed between us. Though she was polite we found little to say to one another. I could see for myself that she was having a hard life; and we both knew that Vienna was suffering from a cold and hungry winter, afraid of the occupation troops, pessimistic about the future. Marianne did tell me that she was about to get married, but there was little joy in her description of her invalid, penniless ex-soldier.

'I could get a better job,' she said, 'if I weren't tied down by this child. I'll be thankful when he's off my hands. . . the stubborn nuisance.'

Not wanting her to say more I got up.

Paul put aside his book. 'Will you come again?'

'If it's all right with your mother.'

'I don't mind,' said Marianne. 'You can come any time you like. It's all the same to me.'

As I went along the bomb-damaged passages, down the dank stone stairs, I made plans for feeding what was left of my family. I'd heard that one could order regular food parcels from Dublin. I'd find out how and where.

I was leaving the tenement when Paul came running after me. 'Madelaine . . . are you going back to England?'

'Not for a long time. I'm working in Vienna.'

'With the English?'

'Yes.'

'Will you take me to England with you? Not now. I mean, when I'm free.'

Suddenly I remembered the night my parents had quarrelled. I remembered what it was like to be a small child, tethered to adults, too young to be allowed a will of one's own, unfree.

Paul was watching me anxiously. 'My mother won't let me go away until I'm bigger . . . She says, she always does her duty. I'm her duty. But she doesn't want me . . . Will you take me to England?'

'Yes Paul, when you're bigger.'

'Promise.'

'It's a promise.'

'Am I your duty Madelaine?'

'No Paul, you're not my duty. You're my own cousin,

and I'll visit you very often because I want to.'

Alex, who was still in the army in Vienna at the time, came with me when I visited Paul and loved him as much as I did. We both realized how right Paul had been about his mother. From his birth she'd kept Paul, looked after him well and even catered to his uncommonly strong intellectual needs. She'd done her best because it was not in her nature to be less than conscientious. Nor was it in her nature to love her child.

When Alex and I returned home and got married Paul wrote to us regularly. And for his sake we went back to Vienna time and again until his mother felt that she'd discharged her duty and could pass Paul on to us.

A room in our cottage was ready for him.

Thinking of the boy who'd chosen us as his parents I'd said good-bye to Miss Frederica lightheartedly.

Three weeks later, still in a happy mood, we were on our way home. The train was chugging into the high mountains of the Arlberg pass when Alex handed me the copy of the Times he'd bought at the station in Vienna.

'Miss Frederica,' he said.

It was the announcement of her death. Suddenly. At her home. Aged eighty-nine. Her last wish denied. Her age revealed.

If only I hadn't told Paul so much about Miss Frederica, Tiger and Mufoo! They'd been an important part of the life he was going to share with us. But I knew, almost as soon as we'd landed at Dover, that there was no need to worry. Paul was busy comparing his dreams of England with reality, and he soon decided that the reality was more exciting.

As our train travelled into Sussex he told us that his Austrian teachers had misinformed him; the country was not as flat as he'd been led to believe, nor as industrialized; there were more trees and more farms.

'Look,' he pointed to a flock of sheep, 'there's a black one. It must be a bastard, like me.'

As night fell he kept his eyes on the sky. 'What a lot of

stars we have in England! I suppose there were stars over Vienna, but I never saw them because of the street lights.'

At home Kathy was awaiting us with a hot meal. And there were two visitors, Miss Ethel, the painter with a new black poodle puppy. The shy, sensitive old lady had come to cushion us against the shock of Miss Frederica's death.

In Paul's room there was a surprise for us all, Miss Ethel's gift of a painting, a serene Sussex summer landscape.

Sussex summer landscape by Miss Ethel Rawlins

Paul was obviously delighted with it. 'Will it stay in my room?'

'It's for you,' Miss Ethel assured him.

'I'm going to be an artist too,' he announced. 'But with a camera. And I'll become a colour printer.'

A line from Goethe's Faust came into my head, *and new life arises from the ruins.* Miss Frederica and her animals were dead; Paul had arrived; Paul was growing up. As I listened to him, explaining to us the processes of colour printing, it occurred to me that he and Miss Frederica would have understood one another well. 'You'll have no difficulties with this boy,' she'd have told me. 'He's quite made up his mind . . .'

On my desk I found a small parcel from Miss Frederica's solicitor. In it was an antique brooch in its original red leather case. I'd once admired its exquisite workmanship and Miss Frederica had told me that it had been the last gift from her fiance before he'd been killed in the Battle of the Somme. A moonstone heart, surrounded by pearls, which Miss Frederica had always worn at her throat. There was also a note in her firm, elegant handwriting; *A keepsake for saving my bacon, literally, on so many happy occasions.*

CHAPTER FIVE

The cottage next door, neglected, riddled with woodworm but structurally sound, had stood empty for several months when I received a telephone call from a village acquaintance.

'A friend of mine is interested in Miss Frederica's cottage. But she's put off by the state it's in. If she could see your home — it's rather similar, isn't it? — she'd see what could be done next door . . . Her name is Renée. She recently lost her husband . . . He died of cancer. Now there are just the two of them, Renée and her boy, Richard. She does want to move to a smaller house and the cottage would be ideal. May I bring her along? She's with me now.'

I took an immediate liking to Renée. The few lines in her heart-shaped face had been formed by laughter. The expression in her eyes — clear, dark brown eyes, slightly turned down at the outer corners — was frank and a little puzzled. The contrast between a childlike quality and her smart brown suit, a dress and jacket which Miss Frederica would have called *ladylike,* explained itself as soon as she spoke. Renée came from Switzerland and her accent was as French as her dress-sense.

After Renée and Luisa had inspected our house I made coffee. Back in the living room Renée was saying that she was going to buy the place next door, now that she'd seen how charming a similar cottage could look.

'Would you mind if I decorated it like yours?' she asked.

'Not at all.'

'The white passages and woodwork makes it look so spacious. But I'll try not to copy your colour schemes in the rooms. My trouble is that I don't have much imagination.'

'Rubbish,' said Luisa. 'She's always had gorgeous homes.'

'It was Dick who had all the ideas . . . Do you remember

the bar he made in our house in Bangkok? Out of an old rickshaw. Remember the night your husband leaned on it?' Suddenly Renée threw back her head and shouted with laughter. It was so infectious that Luisa and I had to join in. 'Muir . . . rested his elbows and . . . and the bar shot right across the lounge. Oh, I'm sorry . . . I'm making such a lot of noise.'

'It's a nice noise,' I told her.

'My God!' Again that deep, whole-hearted laughter. 'You'll soon change your mind if we become neighbours. . . Dick used to say that we could never live in an apartment because I'd soon get arrested for committing a breach of the peace.'

'Dick was fun,' said Luisa. 'When we were out East together . . .'

One way or another the two women had been together for a long time. They'd been students and later nurses at Guy's Hospital. By chance they'd both married men who had run plantations in the Far East. During the war they'd fled from the advancing Japanese. Later both families had returned to England and settled in Sussex within ten miles of one another. Renée's husband had tragically died, yet Renée was obviously determined to keep alive his sense of gaiety and his warmth. And she was planning ahead. Her son, Richard, was due to go to boarding school, to Winchester, his father's and his grandfather's school. She would buy Miss Frederica's cottage, modernize and decorate it, move in and then take up voluntary work at a local hospital.

'Richard isn't keen on my doing a job,' she told me. 'He wants a dog, and he wants me to stay at home and look after it.'

'Perhaps he'd accept a kitten,' I suggested.

'I think he would. What a good idea! Oh . . . I wonder . . . I don't want to be unfair to him.'

'Miss Frederica had a theory that dog-lovers can be very fond of cats. It's cat-lovers who rarely take to other domestic animals.'

The cottage next door, stripped, scrubbed, dewoodwormed and painted smelled sweet and looked good. In went a fine mixture of English and continental furniture — Swiss antique chairs with hand-embroidered seats and backs, a Chippendale desk and table, pleasant oil paintings of Swiss and English ancestors. In most rooms there were objects from the East, Chinese horses, Burmese enamel plates, pots or table lamps. Renée had made the cottage her own and it was a pleasant place to be in.

We also enjoyed our new neighbours' noises; Renée clip-clopping fast along her garden-paths — in Scholl sandals, Renée's gusts of laughter, *Richard! My God! Look at you, you're covered in mud! Mum! Where have you put my football boots? Mu-um! Mon dieu . . . quel enfant! Mum, if you've got to yell, yell in English! Mum, I'm just going next door! I want to show Paul my camera.* A wild rush upstairs, down and through the garden, *back in a minute mum, and can we have baked beans for supper? Mon Dieu! Richard, will you never learn about food? No, mum. I'm half English. See!*

One day Richard, a tall eleven-year old, came into my kitchen at half speed, and gently put before me a fluffy pale grey kitten with golden eyes. 'Madelaine, this is Mitsi. She's an English long-haired cat, not a Persian. . . I wanted a dog. But Mitsi's rather terrific, isn't she?'

Paul came in from one of his photographic expeditions. 'A cat!' He fondled Richard's pet. 'I had a tabby when I was little . . . Well, she really belonged to neighbours, but she used to stay with me when my mother was at work . . . She wasn't as soft as yours.'

Richard passed the kitten to Paul. 'Mitsi's super. I don't mind having her instead of a dog. I mean, cats don't mind being left alone, so mum will be able to work at the hospital. I suppose mum's got to do something when I'm at Winchester. . . Madelaine, what are you going to do when Paul's away at school?'

'I'll be writing a book.'

'Good, then you'll be at home. Will you keep an eye on Mitsi when mum's out? so she doesn't get lost.'

It didn't take Mitsi long to discover the most convenient gap in the hedge between Renée's garden and ours. Like her owners, Mitsi liked life to be well ordered, her days to run to a pattern.

When Renée drove her car out of the garage Mitsi, aware that she'd be deprived of human company for hours, would make for the hole in the hedge. Totally indifferent to her own kind, Mitsi needed people. As there was a bed of flowers and shrubs between our side of the hedge and our cottage, Mitsi remained invisible until she arrived at my kitchen door. But her progress between hedge and door could be charted by the minute stirring of leaves and twigs as she picked her way through the minature jungle, never breaking a stem or flattening a flower.

Mitsi

While working upstairs I always left the kitchen door open. I couldn't keep Mitsi out of her second home even if it did mean more frequent visits from papa-screamer and a bigger booze-bill.

At first Alex had felt dubious about the addition to our family. Once or twice he'd had to help blind Mufoo down a tree and he'd been scratched in the process. But Mitsi never extended a claw to any human. Nor did she swarm up curtains or draw threads out of rugs and upholstery. She had perfect manners, getting up when Alex arrived home, making ceremonial circles of welcome around his legs, purring when stroked. Before long I discovered Alex putting milk in her bowl, which is no way of rebuffing a cat. And Mitsi, spending the occasional evening with us, would make herself comfortable on Alex's lap and allow him to rest his book or medical journal on her back.

For the next couple of years I found myself listening for the sounds of Mitsi's paws galloping upstairs, for the faint creaking of the door as she stalked into the study to take her place on the couch beside my desk.

Only once did she inflict an injury. Normally the voice of papa-screamer sent her ducking under the bookshelves. But on one occasion, when she'd been fast asleep, she was still on the couch when the screamer entered. She was lying on *his* seat. He was about to brush her off, rather crudely, when Mitsi — unaccustomed to such bad manners — turned and bit his thumb.

The screamer, blanching at the sight of a tiny drop of blood, demanded instant antiseptic treatment. 'There's something wrong with this cat . . . It might be infectious.' He was panic-stricken. 'Good heavens! I might catch something ghastly like glandular fever.'

'Don't be silly. Mitsi's perfectly healthy.'

'Oh no, she isn't . . . Dear me, I do feel peculiar . . . Dreadful animal! Don't you know she's got a lump on her side.'

Mitsi did not object to the medical examination. As Alex moved and squeezed the small lump on her flank, she purred ecstatically. A new game? Great.

Nothing to worry about. The lump was a lipoma, a harmless fatty growth which occurs in humans as well as animals. Sometimes such growths are surgically removed for cosmetic reasons. But, provided they cause no discomfort, it's perfectly safe to leave them alone. Mitsi's lipoma was neither uncomfortable nor unsightly. We decided not to mention it to Renée.

But Renée discovered the lump. She came in one morning extremely upset. Her husband's death from cancer had made her very nervous of any kind of growth. I tried to reassure her, explaining what Alex had diagnosed, telling her that the lipoma was such an unimportant little thing that we'd forgotten to mention it to her.

I believed I'd succeeded in putting her mind at rest. I should have known better. When she returned in the evening I realized how much her natural cheerfulness had masked doubts and anxieties.

'I've taken Mitsi to the vet,' she told Alex and me. There were tears in her eyes. 'He says it's cancer.'

'Then he doesn't know what he's talking about,' said Alex. 'How did he examine Mitsi?'

'He just felt the lump with his fingers.'

'No laboratory tests?'

'No. That would take time, wouldn't it?'

'Of course. If that vet thinks that Mitsi has cancer he should be made to prove it scientifically. I am convinced that proper tests would show that the growth is non-malignant.'

Alex went and fetched a textbook. He read to us all there was on lipoma.

At last Renée was laughing with relief. 'I'm such a fool. You're right. I'm sure you are. I don't know what made me take Mitsi to the vet . . . I'll phone him.'

'I shouldn't bother.'

'But I must go and fetch Mitsi.'

'You left her at the vet's?'

'Well, yes. He suggested it. He told me that Mitsi should be put to sleep. I said I couldn't decide; I wanted to talk it over with medical friends and phone him later.'

'Call him now.'

Renée went to the telephone in the hall. We heard the murmur of her voice. We heard the wind buffet the cypresses, the spring rain pound the windows.

'I'll collect Mitsi,' suggested Alex. 'It's been a bad day for Renée.'

And then she was standing in the doorway. 'Oh my God!'

We were waiting for the usual sequel to that exclamation, a funny little story, presumably about Mitsi.

'He said . . .' Renée was not invoking her deity of fun and wonder; her face was very white. 'He said . . . it was a misunderstanding. He thought . . . He's put her to sleep . . . A misunderstanding.'

In the heat of August the flowerbed had filled tightly. Dahlias of every colour had interlaced. The buddleia, in a cloud of butterflies, was sprawling over the Russian vine. In between the gladioli were shooting straight towards the sun, their heavy buds showing the first tips of yellow, white and scarlet.

Was there a movement in this summer jungle? Not for the first time I watched and waited. But of course there was no chain of movements; Mitsi's mischievous golden eyes did not suddenly peer at me from a thicket of flowers.

'I don't understand you people,' said screamer, irritably.

Annoying for him. There he was, strolling about our garden, expecting me to administer the usual psycho-therapy, and I wasn't playing the game. I was paying no attention to his complaints.

'What I mean, don't you see . . .'

I was seeing Richard and Paul, their faces turned to the gap in the hedge, watching, waiting for Mitsi to emerge, and gradually remembering. This sad illusion was troubling all of us, including Alex.

'I mean, the cat's been dead for months.' The screamer, sensitive to receiving less than his usual measure of dry martini and sympathy, had made a shrewd guess. 'It's ridiculous to squander love on an animal.'

'One doesn't *squander* love. One either loves or one doesn't love.'

'I don't see . . .'

'Don't ask me to explain.'

'I say! Shall I mix you another drinkie?'

'No thanks.'

'Tell you what, Madelaine. I'll have a word with Renée . . . I'll ask her to give you a kitten for your birthday.'

'You'll do nothing of the sort.' Driven into a corner by the screamer, I blurted out, 'We're going to have a dog.'

CHAPTER SIX

When Alex had asked me what I wanted for my birthday I'd been certain that my present should be a coffee-coloured long-haired miniature dachshund. In the morning I felt just as certain that my night of recollection had been constructive, that it would make me a more welcoming and understanding dog-owner. I'd learned that my good relationships with people or animals depend largely on self-knowledge, on the painstakingly sought insight that makes one sensitive to the motives and feelings of other creatures.

Over breakfast I told Alex a little about Gruber, but also about dachshunds I'd met since. There'd been John Bowen's little bitch, gracefully curled up on his lap, sleeping through the committee meetings of a Writers' Club. And John Pertwee's dachs, sitting between us while we discussed a filmscript of one of my books, small head turning from one to the other of us, trying extremely hard to follow the drift of the conversation. As to the dachshunds in our lane, Miss Joy's menagerie, Alex had seen them often enough.

'And, of course, there was Mitsi,' said Alex thoughtfully. 'It may be a good idea not to have another cat.'

'Do you mean a dog *is* a good idea?'

'I didn't say so.' He smiled. 'But that won't stop you going on a puppy-hunt. If you don't find a dog you want in time, don't worry. No reason why you shouldn't wait until Christmas or next August.'

No reason. But I didn't want to wait. The moment Alex's car was out of sight I made for the telephone.

Miss Joy was very helpful. She had shown some of her dachshunds at Cruft's and knew all the best breeders. 'If you drop in — any time this morning — I'll give you a list.'

I allowed her less than an hour to prepare it.

No one approaching her cottage could doubt that it was owned by the dachshunds. High on a grassy mound the large long-haired senior, who had taken it upon himself to alert the whole family every time anyone dared pass within twenty yards of him, gave his deep and impressive bark. It called forth a deafening chorus throughout cottage and garden. That the window sills were manned by dachsies was obvious; their barks, ranging from the highest c-sharp to bottom b-flat, so agitated the net curtains that they looked as if a gale were blowing inside the house.

Miss Joy, buffeted by dachsunds of all sizes, opened the door and invited me in. 'Shoosh, all of you!' she yelled.

The dogs barked on.

'Will you shut up or not?' The dogs' voices lost some of the assertiveness.

'Lesson one,' said Miss Joy. 'When you have a dachsy you've got to do a lot of face-saving. Your face. Don't ever say, *Come here*; it's got to be *Will you come here or not.* Dachsies are congenitally disobedient. That's why it's wise to leave your options open. If you say, *Will you shut up or not* your dachs will shut up or not, but you won't have lost face. And of course, if you don't want to lose all hope of ever controlling your dachs, you mustn't lose face.'

'Sounds complicated.'

'Not a bit, Madelaine. Living with a dachsy is no more and no less difficult than living with a man. I've tried both. I'd say dachsies are more rewarding. Unlike men they have strong affections and few ulterior motives. Here,' she took a sheet of paper from her pocket. 'I've listed the breeders whose dogs I know personally.'

She went on to explain the letters beside each name and address. R.I.B.A. did not stand for Royal Institute of British Architects but Red (colour of dog), Inbred (slightly), Bark (on the loud side), Above Average Price. Q.C. meant Quiet Animals, Colours Various. M.D. stood for Much in Demand (hence, hard to get hold of). And O.B.E. did not mean the honour conferred by the monarch but the kennel's Outstanding Breeding Experience.

Miss Joy gave me a final tip. 'When you enquire about

pups you mustn't mention *coffee-colour* . . . or the breeder will know that you're ignorant and sell you one of her less good dogs. There's no such thing as a coffee-coloured dachshund. Coffee-coloured dachsies are called *red*.'

Our local telephone operator became very interested in my quest. 'Is this another dog breeder you're calling?'

I said it was.

'Oh, I know. It's Mrs Brendan's number. No good phoning her before six o'clock. I've just seen her go down the road. Expect she's gone to tea at her daughter's. . . Now, where else shall we try?'

I gave her a Bristol number.

'That's far away. I mean, if they have a puppy, how are you going to get it home?'

'By car, I suppose.'

'But some dogs get ever so sick in cars. I once had a puppy . . .'

'Please will you get me Bristol . . .'

'I'm only trying to help.'

'I know. It's very good of you.'

I was becoming disheartened. At Bogside puppies had to be ordered a year in advance. At Littlemead all pups, with the exception of a coughing bitch, had been sold a couple of days earlier. The Berkshire kennels had informed me that their pups normally went abroad, but if they should have a dog in the next litter which wasn't good enough for America they'd consider selling it to me.

At Bristol I also drew a blank. Bristol offered me a place on the kennels' waiting list, which I declined.

'Oh dear,' said the telephone operator, 'what are we going to do?'

'We'll keep trying. I've got another couple of breeders on my list.'

'Why don't you get a stray? The R.S.P.C.A. are bound to have one. I mean, you don't have to have a dachshund, do you? Meself, I think mongrels are ever so much nicer. I once had a mongrel . . .'

'Would you mind very much if I tried Hurst? The number is . . .'

'It's all right with me. . . if you want to waste your money.'

The woman who answered at Hurst shouted down the line. 'Will you speak up please! I'm deaf. Very deaf.'

I spoke up. The answering silence lasted so long that I wondered whether my request had been comprehended. I was about to repeat it when the line came alive.

'I've got a pencil.' The woman sounded quite businesslike. 'I want a few details. Name . . . Address . . . Telephone number . . . Right. Husband's profession?'

I thought she was going a little too far, but I told her that my husband was a doctor.

'Well, I might be able to help you.' Suddenly the voice sounded silky with charm. 'It's difficult to find what you want at such short notice. As it happens I have no puppies at the moment. But one of the dogs I sold last year is available. He went to a family who can't cope with him . . . I don't mean Kim's difficult. Not at all. It's just . . . there's been a lot of trouble in the family. The husband . . . he's a farmer . . . had an accident. Broke his leg. So the wife has to look after him. And she isn't very strong. Their daughter's in hospital, having a baby, and the grandchildren are staying at the farm. The youngest fell down and broke a tooth . . .'

The tale of troubles became so complicated and dramatic that I finished up believing none of it.

'. . . and that's why they've decided to part with Kim. Now; Kim's had all his injections. He's a strong, healthy black and tan and . . .'

'But it's a red I want,' I shouted.

'He's house trained of course.' The woman ignored my objection. 'And as he isn't a puppy . . . he's fourteen months old . . . they're selling him cheap. Fifteen pounds. It's a great bargain. Normally any pup I've bred costs eighty.'

That much was true. My earlier phone calls had given me an idea of prices. For a long-haired miniature dachshund even eighty pounds was not unreasonable. Fifteen was much nearer the price I'd envisaged. But even at a bargain price, what would Alex say to a puppy which was a full grown dog of the wrong colour?

'I'm sorry. I don't think . . .'

'You're very lucky,' Mrs Hurst cut in. 'As it happens I'm driving down your way on Friday . . . Tell you what I'll do. I'll bring Kim along . . .'

Friday was my birthday. A good omen? No, I wasn't going to fall for that one. 'I don't think Kim's what I want,' I said firmly. 'So please don't bother . . .'

'Wait!' shouted Mrs Hurst. 'You'll see the dog next Friday. It's settled. But I promise you, if you don't like Kim I'll take him away.' And down went her receiver.

'Well? What are we going to do now?' asked the operator. 'Hadn't I better re-connect you?'

'No thanks.'

'What's the next number on your list?'

'I'm not going to call any more breeders.'

'You letting that woman have it all her own way?'

'I don't know.' I felt I'd been foolish and weak.

'I mean, it's all the same to me,' said the operator. 'But Kim isn't a puppy, is he?

'No.'

'Not even the colour you want.'

'I know.'

'If I were you I'd call back and tell that woman you don't want her second-hand dog.'

'No point. She's deaf.'

'Deaf, my foot! She'd no trouble hearing your name and address. She's just like an auntie of mine . . .'

'Well, thanks very much . . .'

'Never heard what she didn't want to hear. Always got her own way, did auntie . . . I bet that dog-woman's taking you for a ride.'

'She did say she'd take the dog away if I didn't like him.'

'Sales-talk . . . And all this blarney about *as it happens* she's driving down your way on Friday. Bet she's making a special journey . . . a long one too. I mean, you can see she wants to get rid of that dog.'

'The dog isn't hers. Don't you think it's nice of her to take so much trouble . . .'

'Trouble? Bet that dog's trouble . . . Well, it's all the same to me, but don't say I didn't warn you.'

CHAPTER SEVEN

The day of the dog dawned; wet, very wet. Never before had it rained on my birthday. Having told Alex that I'd found the perfect puppy, I was feeling uneasy and the rain made me even more subdued.

'You're still young,' said Alex, misunderstanding my silence. 'Sorry I have no birthday present for you yet.'

'It'll arrive.'

'You've got some food for it?'

'I'll cook ox-cheek.'

'Is that right for a puppy?'

'Well . . . yes. Kim wasn't born yesterday.'

'I'll get the dog basket on my way to the hospital,' he promised.

'And a collar and lead?'

'Yes. But what size of collar?'

'The smallest you can get.'

He shook his head. 'Perhaps you should have got a labrador after all.'

I watched Alex drive off. In the lane Mr Cox, the husband of Miss Frederica's former help and our local street sweeper, was sheltering under a tree. The rain was making his job difficult and I felt sorry for him. I opened the door and asked him into the kitchen for a cup of coffee.

'Thank you kindly.' He kicked off his boots at the door. 'Never so weary, never so in woe,' he declaimed in a fine baritone voice, 'Bedabbled with the dew and torn with briers . . . Shakespeare.'

'Lovely.'

'Midsummer-Night's Dream.' Mr Cox held out a hand for his cup of coffee. 'If it be mine keep it not from me; quickly let me have it . . . Bet you don't know where this quotation comes from, ma'am.'

'No. Shakespeare?'

'Who but the bard, ma'am? Macbeth.' He took a sip. 'Ah! But might I of Jove's nectar sup . . . And that's Ben Jonson. And he was no fool neither. Time was when the Drama Society in this village was great. There was King Lear, and though I say it myself there's been many a Lear worse'n me. We got the County drama award for my Lear . . . Well, the Society isn't what it used to be. All them modern plays. Mind you, ma'am, I'm not saying there isn't any talent now. Are you going to join the Drama Society?'

'No Mr Cox. I'm a ham.'

'How about your doggie then? Prudence, the telephone girl that is, says you're going to have a little doggie . . . There's going to be a puppy in our next play.'

'Perhaps we'd better wait and see whether the pup's acting material.'

'Nothing like starting early in acting, ma'am.' He set down his empty cup. 'I hope you'll be pleased with the new doggie. He should be all right on stage anyway, seeing as he's going to be a literary pup . . . Thank you kindly for the refreshment . . . I do believe the rain has stopped.' He went to the door and pulled on his boots. 'By the fire that quickens Nilus' slime,' he declaimed, 'I go from hence Thy soldier, servant . . .'

'Antony and Cleopatra.'

'My ears discern a carriage at the gate; forsooth the doggie is not late. Instant poetry by Lancelot Cox. Farewell.'

The carriage, which had just hit our gatepost, was a muddy and battered vintage Morris. Its driver was not, as I'd expected, an elderly country woman in tweeds but a middle aged girl in a frilly flowered nylon dress, white gloves and men's gumboots. She was holding a bundle done up in gift-wrap paper and a large pale blue bow.

'Your telephone operator let me know.' She was examining me, gravely, from top to toe. 'Happy birthday.' The wrapping-paper wriggled. A split appeared in the parcel and—in the gap— a brown eye which seemed much too large for a small dog.

Portrait of Sir Timothy Hemjoy as a young dog

Mrs Hurst followed me into the living room. Looking at her, perched on the edge of the couch, I liked what I saw. Looking at the gift-wrapped parcel, I remembered Prudence's warning; *I bet that dog-woman's taking you for a ride.*

'As I told you on the phone,' said Mrs Hurst. 'Kim's had the wrong kind of home.' The parcel was shivering on her lap. 'I'd have liked to keep him a bit longer . . . get him into prime condition again . . . but as you wanted him so much . . .'

'I don't yet know whether I want him.'

'Soon see.' She tore open the paper and extracted a skinny dachshund. Put on its feet, the animal pressed close to the carpet and slunk under the nearest chair. I'd never seen a more miserable little runt.

As I looked at it a large stain spread moistly around its trembling body, soaking into my pale turquoise carpet.

'Soon put this right,' said Mrs Hurst, brisquely. 'Got any sodawater?'

'Yes.'

'Get it. Quickly . . . Good girl.'

Taking the bottle from me, she got on her knees and began to squirt sodawater on the stain. The dog fled, under another chair.

'Now a cloth,' she ordered. 'Better make it a big one.'

The cloth was pushed at the carpet with short, hard jabs which reduced the moisture surprisingly well.

Mrs Hurst dropped the wet rag on the hearth. 'Don't ask me why, but sodawater prevents permanent staining. Works like magic. Well now . . .'

'You said the dog was house-trained.'

'So he is,' she asserted. But he doesn't yet know this house, does he?'

'If this is how he's going to behave every time I take him to a strange house, he's not going to be very popular.'

'I promised to take him away,' Mrs Hurst was trying to keep her temper, 'and I will, if you don't like him.'

The dog and I gazed at one another. He was showing too much of the whites of his eyes. A hysterical dog? I certainly didn't want a problem pup. But what beautiful, large eyes! What an awful coat though! The animal, which should have been thickly covered in silky hair was half naked. And he wasn't really black and tan; rather a blackish brown and cream. The poor state of his coat apart, his markings were nice; pale gold paws, cream shirt-front, pale gold lower half of face contrasting well with dark upper half, small gold circles above the eyes, round gold ear rings on the cheeks.

I got down on the floor. 'Kimmy nice dog. Come here. . . come on.' The tail, which should have been a proud plume but was a thin rat's tail, wagged; tentatively.

Suddenly I saw a louse wander slowly from the middle of the dog's head to his left ear.

Mrs Hurst had seen it too. 'Nothing to worry about. Another dose of DDT will get rid of the livestock. I've brought some with me.'

'All this and lice too.' I felt I should tell Mrs Hurst to take the little runt away. Yet I couldn't bring myself to do it; the eyes of the dog held so much consciousness, such concentration. Kim was trying so hard to understand the connection between Mrs Hurst and me.

I said, 'I'll have him.'

'I thought you would. You won't regret it. He's in poor condition now, I'm not denying it, but he's a champion. He was one of my best pups. He's registered at the Kennel Club as Sir Timothy Hemjoy.'

Well, the aristocracy had its runts. But I thought of the letters Miss Joy had scribbled beside Mrs Hurst's address. O.B.E. — for outstanding breeding experience. I stopped distrusting the frilly, gum-booted woman and went to fetch the blank cheque Alex had given me.

I had separated the Morris's bumper and our gatepost and watched Mrs Hurst rattle off towards Brighton. Sir Timothy Hemjoy was still hiding under the chair in the living room, looking petrified. The louse had reached his forehead. I felt tempted to use the DDT, but on second thought it seemed wrong to embarrass the dog so early in our relationship. The destruction of the louse could wait until we'd become better acquainted.

Kim was gazing at the lead Mrs Hurst had given me, not with enthusiasm. It was the kind of thing that slipped over a dog's head, choked the animal if it walked too fast or became too slack when it stopped.

'Sorry Kim, it's the only lead I've got just now.' I'd always talked to animals and I hoped that Sir Timothy too would listen. 'Shall we go for a walk?'

The dog wriggled forward, just a few inches.

'Look Kim, you've been in the car four hours. I'm not blaming your for making a puddle. But you'll disgrace yourself again if we don't go out.' I jingled the lead. 'Coming?'

Kim abandoned his hiding place. He was shivering, but he allowed me to slip the lead over his head.

The rain-clouds had dispersed and a hot sun was drawing out the scents of grass and honeysuckle, clover and meadowsweet. The dog trotted beside me, head down, tail tucked under, a depressed and timorous dachs.

We turned off the lane into a twitten of smallholdings and little cottage. At the gate of the local witch, a weird Irish woman, sat her big marmalade cat. Kim gave a cry of fear, which sounded human, pressed closer to the ground and emptied his bladder.

'You *are* a dog, I hope.' I took a look. 'Yes, I'm sure you are. So why aren't you lifting a leg like other dogs?'

Kim pulled forward and choked on the lead. His one idea was to get away from the witch's cat. We reached the main road, walked on a couple of hundred yards, and turned left into the field behind Martin-and-Wendy's house. Strolling towards us, through the high grass, came Wendy's black Persian cat, Sooty.

Kim quivered and stopped. Sooty had reached the path and was coming to meet us. She was one of those happy, gentle cats who got on well with all living things from people to cows and dogs. Confident of a welcome she approached the still little dog until her nose touched his. As she rubbed her cheek against Kim's the dog's tail rose and wagged. I was pleased that Kim knew how to discriminate between the wild fighting cat belonging to the witch and the sweet-natured Sooty.

We wandered on along the path, Sooty and Kim side by

side. Raindrops were glittering on the buttercups. Big blackberries were turning red. The mist had lifted and the high line of the Downs stretched clear against the summer sky. A good birthday after all.

Suddenly there was a commotion in the field and Miss Ethel's poodle came belting out of the tall grass. Kim, seeing those prancing paws, gave his strange cry of fear, backed and slipped his lead. Before I could make a grab he was off, fleeing down the path at an astonishing speed.

He could run much faster than I. Sprinting after him, I saw him dive under the field gate and make for the main road. I slowed down. What was the use? This was almost certainly the end of Kim. The panic-stricken dog wouldn't stand much of a chance in the traffic. But what if he was as good a dog as Mrs Hurst had made out? A clever dog would go back the way he'd come, along the pavement, through the twitten, back to the only house in the village which he knew. Yet, surely, that was asking too much of a small, frightened animal. Kim hadn't been in the village more than an hour; he'd only once walked through twitten and lane.

When I got to the main road there was no sign of the dog. But there was no traffic pile-up either. Walking fast, trying to stifle my hopes, I made a silent promise; if Kim had found his way back to our cottage, despite his panic, I'd never again question his quality. I'd believe in his courage and intelligence no matter what he did.

I so much wanted to find Kim, yet when I did it seemed a miracle. He was cowering against our gate, still trembling, still showing the white of his eyes, yet making no attempt to run away from me.

Kim followed me into the kitchen and lay down on the mat beside the door. I poured milk into a bowl and put it in front of him. Mrs Hurst had said that the dog mightn't want a meal for twenty-four hours but that he'd never refuse milk.

Kim didn't exactly refuse; he just ignored the proffered dish. I dipped a finger in the milk and held it out for him to lick. The dog showed no interest; he just lay there as dejected as ever.

'Kimmy, you're supposed to be mad about milk.' I sat down on the mat beside him. He flinched but didn't flee. 'Come on,' I pleaded, 'just a mouthful. You must be thirsty.'

I moved the milk towards him

No reaction.

'Just as well that Paul and Richard are away. They'd be disappointed in you. . . Of course I know you're a clever little dog . . . Come on, have a drink. Please. Kim, what shall I do with you? Shall I tell you a story?'

I told him about Roger the ladybird. I told him about my other pets; the foxcub, Lady Hamilton, which I'd brought up after its mother had been killed by a plough; the lizard, Effie, which I'd nursed back to health after some animal had bitten off its tail. I told Kim that Paul and Richard had gone visiting friends in Scotland and described the house on Loch Rannoch, the mountains, the lake, the fishing.

Kim kept me talking, beside him on the kitchen floor, for a couple of hours or more before he lifted his head and looked me in the face, gingerly, as if he were a wild animal, I moved the milk towards his nose. 'Come on Kimmy. Have your milk. I won't watch you.'

I got up very slowly and quietly and went to fetch a book. When I returned Kim was on his feet contemplating the milk, and as I walked out into the garden I heard — with relief — that he was drinking.

It seemed wise to leave him alone, to let him explore the cottage undisturbed. I took a garden chair into the sun and began to read a novel I'd saved up for a day when I wouldn't be able to work. But my thoughts soon strayed to live people, to the old friends who'd sent me birthday cards. Some of them were heading for trouble.

There had been chill undercurrents when I'd seen Vicky and her family in Canada. Was Vicky's marriage breaking up? If so, what would happen to her children, Quentin and Rose? The family hadn't been in Canada long enough to make close friends. I anticipated that Vicky and the children would return to England. But they no longer had a house to return to. Vicky would have to find a new teaching job. It would take her time to make a new home. Our cottage was too small to accommodate three extra people. Should we be looking for a larger house?

And then there was the Bock family in California.

Though Charles Bock was ten years older than I, our friendship went back to my childhook in Neustadt. After the Nazis take-over in 1938 Charles had fled to Yugoslavia. Driven on by the war, he'd joined an uncle in Japan. He had met his wife there, the daughter of an American medical missionary. Eventually the Bocks had settled in California. Charles and Felicia had two daughters and a son of sixteen. They were worrying about their boy, Jimmy. The war in Vietnam was dragging on; it was likely that Jimmy would become yet another American victim of political lunacy. If he got into a university his army service might be deferred, but unfortunately Jimmy wasn't doing well at school. Should Alex and I invite Jim to stay with us? Suggest to his parents that an English school might help him produce better results?

I hadn't yet discussed the Jimmy-idea with Alex. Perhaps my birthday was the time to broach the subject. Alex would, of course, trot out every argument against transplanting the boy. But in the end he'd agree that it might be a case of saving Jimmy's life.

Oh people! They certainly slowed down my writing. Yet my one experience of working in *perfect* conditions — when I'd been awarded an Authors' Fellowship in America — had proved that ivory towers were not for me. Free from chores, such as cooking and looking after a family, I should have written faster and better. Should have. But didn't.

So here I was, in our garden on a hot August day, dreaming of a future full of other people's children; almost certainly nine year old Quentin, twelve year old Rose and sixteen year old Jimmy, not to speak of Paul. But our Paul was easy, warm-hearted, never bored and making straight for his desired profession. Soon Paul would be off to a college for graphics and printing.

I had almost forgotten the dog when I became aware of soft ticking sounds. Sir Timothy Hemjoy was on the move, timorously pawing his way along the brick path. He stopped at my chair, eyes large and solemn.

'Hello,' I welcomed him. 'Feeling better?'

Down went his head, shyly, not stubbornly.

'What do you want? Shall I tell you more stories?'

Kim gave a deep sigh. Suddenly his muscles tensed. He launched himself into the air and landed on my lap.

'I've got the dog gear,' Alex announced. 'Where's the dog?'

'Under my chair.' The arrival of the car had sent Kim into hiding.

Alex lay down on the lawn. 'Good God! Is that the animal of your choice?'

'Of course . . . He's just a bit shy.'

'Aren't puppies supposed to be plump?'

'Some aren't.'

'This one's very skinny. It hasn't much of a coat either.'

'Kim's too young to have a thick coat.'

'I see. There's never been a pup like him . . . What about his colour? I thought you wanted a coffee-coloured dachs. If I'm not mistaken, this one's black.'

'He isn't. He's mocca.'

'After-dinner coffee with whipped cream, I suppose . . . He looks whipped all right. Scared silly.'

'He's had a long journey. And he's in a new place. That's all. He came and sat on my lap.'

'A real hero . . . Are you itchy?'

'Me?'

'Yes you, Madelaine. Unless I've forgotten my zoology the insect on your dog's shirt front is a louse.'

The moment of truth had come. I told Alex the whole story, from my telephone calls to Kim's flight from the field, from the story-telling session on the kitchen floor to Kim's going to sleep on my lap.

'Kim's no fool,' I pleaded.

'We'll see.' Alex reached for the dog.

'Don't!' I grabbed his arm.

'What now? I just want to see the animal.'

'You'll have to wait for him to come to you.'

'Is it that bad?'

'Yes. I had my doubts about the story Mrs Hurst told

me. I think I know now what really happened to Kim.'

'Ill treated.'

'Very. His breeder found out somehow and did her best to rescue him.'

'Well, she's certainly succeeded. If you hadn't fallen for this bundle of misery, she might well have offered you something better. Aren't you sorry?'

'No.'

'All right . . . I'll get the dog basket out of the car.'

I wondered how Kim would react if I removed the sheltering chair. Would he panic? Would he allow me to pick him up? I didn't believe that Kim's jumping on my lap had been a declaration of complete confidence.

Leaving the dog under my chair, I got up and wandered indoors. After a while Kim slunk into the kitchen and sat down on the mat beside the half empty milkbowl.

Alex came in with a collar and lead, which looked about the right size, and a wicker basket which seemed small even for a miniature dachs.

He put the basket on the floor. 'Perhaps I should have got the next size. Kim! Bed!'

The dog glanced at the basket, in the middle of the kitchen, and lowered his head.

I picked it up and put it in the recess between two cupboards. 'I usually sit with my back to the wall. Guess Kim does.'

'Primitive defensive position.'

I hadn't yet set the basket down when Sir Timothy rose, trotted across the kitchen and jumped straight in. He rolled into a little ball, tucked his nose under his tail and went to sleep.

'That's that.' Alex was pleased with the success of the basket.

'That won't be that,' I warned.

'The lice?'

'They'll be the least of our problems.'

CHAPTER EIGHT

Alex and I had always been a healthily disunited couple. It took Sir Timothy Hemjoy to extend our disagreements to the borderline between amicable argument and real annoyance.

'Have you dusted the dog?'

'No. He hates DDT . . . Anyway, I think the lice have gone.'

'I don't. I don't want lice in the house. You've got to persevere.'

'Well, I'm not going to worry Kim unnecessarily.'

For three days the dog had taken nothing but milk.

'Madelaine, what are you doing on the kitchen floor?'

'Quiet! Kim's almost finished a dish of ox cheek.'

'Decent of him. You aren't hand-feeding him?'

'I am. I can't let him starve to death.'

'He'll eat when he's hungry.'

'He was hungry just now but . . .'

'Are you going to sit on the floor and tell stories every time the dog's supposed to have a meal?'

'We've got to give him time. Remember what kind of a home he came from.'

'I'm not likely to forget, especially if you go on making a fool of yourself.'

I'd read that small dachshunds shouldn't be allowed to climb stairs because they might slip discs or otherwise hurt their backs.

'Alex! Alex! Don't let the dog go upstairs. I've asked you to stop him.'

'Rubbish.'

'Look; our stairs are very steep. For a little thing like Kim it must be like climbing Everest.'

'Don't be silly. I'd let him go up and down as much as he wants; it'll strengthen his muscles.'

'But it says in the book . . .'

'Forget the book. Has he had his dinner?'

'Not yet.'

'All right, I'll give it to him. Don't fuss, Madelaine. And get changed. We're dining in Brighton.'

I'd forgotten. 'I won't go. Tell the Fishers I've got a headache or something.'

'I'll do nothing of the sort . . . You can't stay with the dog forever. He'll have to get used to being left *sometime.*'

'It's too soon . . . I must feed him.'

'I said I'd do it.'

'Then he won't eat.'

For the first time Kim took his food without the story-telling and coaxing. We left him alone in the cottage; with a light on — much to Alex's disgust.

Of course I blamed myself for my thoughtlessness. Why hadn't we taken the dog with us? I'd discovered that he loved travelling and didn't mind being left in the car. And at the dinner party I managed to put the best part of my steak into my handbag, unobserved.

But Alex had noticed. 'Disgusting, wrapping food up in your handkerchief.'

'I just wanted to bring him something . . . You know, Kim still hasn't made a sound. Do you think there's something wrong with his vocal cords?'

'What next! He hasn't yet found anything worth barking at.'

If Kim had heard us enter the cottage, he'd certainly seen no reason for breaking his silence.

'Alex, why is he so quiet.'

'He's probably been busy chewing up my slippers.'

'He's never chewed up a thing . . . Hope nothing's scared him.'

Kim met us at the door between kitchen and dining room. The tail was wagging the whole dog and the dog was emitting quite melodious grunts of pleasure. I'd have hugged Kim for giving us such a welcome if I hadn't been afraid of taking too much for granted. So we just stroked the dog, rather gingerly.

The kitchen was in strange disorder. There'd been a

stack of old newspapers on top of a cupboard, ready for the dustmen. Kim must have leaped high to pull them down and worked hard to spread them around at the back door.

Suddenly Alex burst out laughing. 'It's unbelievable! Come and look at this.'

It was a couple of turds, neatly deposited on a thick wad of newspapers. Obviously Kim had laboured at parcelling them up, but hadn't quite succeeded.

'Kim,' said Alex. 'Sorry I've underrated you. You really are a very clever little animal.'

Not everyone approved of Kim, but no one in the village ignored him.

Sheila, the girl who was our postman, said she didn't trust dogs that didn't bark at her.

Mr Cox, quoting Shakespeare's *dogs of war*, said Kim might eventually do on stage as he wasn't one of them yappy dogs.

Dr Bogey pointed out that Kim looked rather like Marlene Dietrich; same slim face, same long eyelashes.

Martin-and-Wendy's children thought highly of Kim because he had the good sense to be friends with their cat Sooty.

Miss Ethel, the painter, wisely didn't bring her poodle when she called. She looked at our dog with an artist's eye and said he was much the same shape as her vacuum cleaner. When she dropped a piece of biscuit, I called, 'Kimmy! Hoover!' And wonder of wonders, the dog came out from under my chair, ate the biscuit and every crumb in sight. From that moment the word *hoover* became an important and delectable part of Kim's vocabulary and our floors are immaculately crumb-free.

Miss Joy didn't like the look of Kim at all. 'I wish I hadn't recommended Mrs Hurst's kennels. This dog looks awful . . . Poor coat, loose shoulders.'

'Mrs Hurst said that Kim's a champion.'

'She must be out of her mind.'

Kim had been with us a couple of weeks when the screamers returned from their holiday.

Papa, as usual, walked into our garden and yelled at the windows of the study. 'Madelaine! We're back! Dawling, how are you? I'm coming up! Be with you in a jiffy!'

Suddenly I heard angry growls followed by deep-voiced barking. I ran downstairs, expecting to find papa screamer's labrador attacking our Kim. Nothing of the kind. Kim, about the same size as the screamer's shoe, was standing four square at the open back door, barking his head off. It was wonderful to see the screamer held at bay by the little dog with his big bark. At last, at last Sir Timothy had found someone worth barking at.

'I say, dawling,' the screamer kept an eye on Kim. 'What a funny dog! He looks rather dangerous.'

Paul returned from Scotland with fine sketches and photographs, studies of light and shade on mountains and lochs, close-ups of flowers he hadn't seen before. From his earliest days in Britain he'd been fascinated with the wildlife and absorbed in recording it. He called thrushes *troopers*, because they began their evening song with a loud *bloody hell*, and coaltits *little Chinamen*. Crickets, he maintained, sounded like the whistling of a football referee, and he christened frogs *Micawbers* — because he imagined Mr Micawber as a portly gentleman given to belching.

Sir Timothy Hemjoy, who took an instant liking to Paul, became his chippie, short for chipolata sausage. And, of course, Paul discovered more facets to Kim's personality than any one dog could possible display.

'Chippie has a special relationship with the sun,' Paul told us.

True. Indoors Kim would follow the sun all around the house. Out of doors his favourite place was an iron manhole cover which became too hot for me to touch. Yet such heat didn't roast Kim, it made him sigh with satisfaction.

Paul took pictures of Kim defecating under the hedge.

'Compared to dogs, humans look ridiculous; Kim's attractive even when he's squatting.'

By the time Renée and Richard returned from their holiday Kim no longer looked a runt. He'd filled out and his coat, though still on the sparse side, was soft and glossy.

Richard came rushing into our kitchen, 'Madelaine, is it true? The screamers say you've got a dog.'

'That's right.'

'Super! You know, you shared my cat . . . Will you let me share your dog?'

'Of course. But first you'll have to make friends with him.'

He hung around until Paul and Kim returned from the Downs. And then, before I could stop him, Richard made a grab for the dog.

'Hey, gently! You'll scare him. He's nervous with strangers.'

'I'm no stranger . . . Look!' Kim, firmly held in Richard's arms, was nuzzling his ears.

Renée came in, and burst out laughing. 'Oh my God! The size of it!' It *was* funny — little Kim, back on the floor, with the six-foot-plus boys towering above him.

Renée bent to pick up the dog, but Kim escaped under a chair.

'Mum, don't grab,' Richard rebuked. 'You've got to make friends with Kim first . . . Madelaine, will you let him stay with us?'

'Yes, when he's a bit more sure of himself.'

Even after Kim had accepted Renée and Richard as part of our family he still flinched when any of us made a sudden movement.

It was Paul and Richard who devised a treatment for this nervousness. One morning I found the two boys in my study, on their knees on either side of the Victorian couch. Kim was reclining on the couch.

Paul said, 'We've worked it out. What Kim needs is psychiatric treatment.'

'We don't think he's a mental case,' Richard assured

me. 'We've just got to make him self-confident. We've been reading it up.'

'In Alex's textbooks?'

'That's right . . . Watch.'

Kim certainly had enough self-confidence to stay on the couch and lie on his back, anticipating the pleasures of having his chest and stomach rubbed.

'Seconds out!' ordered Richard. 'Box!'

Paul began to jab his fists at Kim, moving fast without actually touching the dog.

Kim flinched. Paul stopped.

'Third round! . . . Box!'

The same performance. I was waiting for Kim to leap off the couch and hide. But he didn't.

'Seconds out! Box!'

The dog was shivering, but he stayed put.

Suddenly, in the tenth round, Kim bared his teeth. He had stopped flinching and he was grinning from ear to ear. Up came his front paws, left, right, left right. He was boxing. He was fighting back.

With the boys away at school. Kim became my constant companion. I had started work on a new book. And so, instead of ten-mile walks over the Downs, Kim had to make do with car-rides, the garden and short runs on the nearby cricket field. But he was not lonely.

Sooty, the black Persian, came almost every day and did her best to teach Kim catcraft. She trained him in stalking and watched with pride when he caught his first mouse. She taught him cat-methods of washing, supervising his toilet and occasionally completing it with a lick behind the ears.

Sooty was less successful with the commando-training. Kim did try to follow her up the trees, but these efforts always ended in a tumble from the lowest branches or a somersault. Kim's contribution to the friendship was rather negative. He strongly disapproved of Sooty's weakness for birds and stopped her, with a menacing growl, from preying on them.

Kim much preferred Sooty to his own species. On our walks he avoided dogs. And no dog was allowed into our cottage, though he would permit visitors to avail themselves of the garden.

Bitches were another matter. He'd put up with them in and out of his house. Occasionally he'd admire a bitch from the distance, trying to arouse her attention with soft barking and a fanning-out of fluffy ears and tail. But Kim's advances, too subtle and lyrical, were usually ignored. Only Lottie, a smooth-haired dachs, was sufficiently interested to touch noses with Kim. As she lived in another village, some eight miles away, Kim was in no position to follow up his first success. Eileen, Lottie's owner, vaguely mentioned the possibility of mating our dogs, but with a busy Christmas season ahead we forgot all about it.

Kim didn't approve of winter. Even the hottest fire didn't compensate him for the real thing, and he pursued the sun with untiring determination. On bright days the sun moved from our bedroom to the living room, from my study to Paul's room. Kimmy followed the cycle, and whenever he discovered the next pool of sunlight on carpet or chair he'd occupy the spot and sniff at it as if the sun had a special scent.

The spring storms, which came blowing from the sea across the Downs, made Kim restless. He loathed getting wet, but the wind drove him into frenzied activity. The wind made great demands on his policing abilities. He'd rush between trees and hedges, frustrated by his failure to stop the perpetual motion of twigs and branches, those blatant breaches of the peace.

One blustery evening Kim was late for his dinner. Alex and I went searching our garden and Renée's. No sign of the dog. By eight o'clock I had visions of Kim shut in a stable at the farm behind our cottage or even caught in a rabbit snare.

We went looking for him on the farm and in the neighbours' gardens. Listening into the howling gale we strained our ears for sounds of a bark or a cry. We tramped miles of fieldpaths and roads, whistling and calling his name, and we climbed in and out of the sandpit beyond the cricket field.

Around three in the morning we gave up. Alex wouldn't let me call the police. What was the use? One couldn't expect a police-force to turn out in the middle of the night for a small black dachsund.

We went to bed, feeling wide awake, weary and worried.

I could not believe that Kim had gone far. He'd never strayed further than Renée's garden. Imagining him in the grip of a fox-trap, hurt, crying for help, I got up again.

Alex grabbed hold of me. 'Madelaine, you're not going out in this storm.'

'Kim's out in it.'

'Well, you've always said he's no fool . . . Back to bed. I won't have you break your neck.'

'We can't just abandon Kimmy.'

'Kimmy's abandoned us.'

CHAPTER NINE

The gale was buffeting the village, tormenting the trees, racketing in our rafters like a delinquent gang. And I was in the grip of nightmares, the ghosts which I'd held at bay — perhaps by living and working to the limits of my energy — for many years.

Nightmares, memories, ghosts have this in common — that they are unfettered by calendar or clock, travelling at random between past and future. Though they are disembodied things, and the dreamer might recognize them for what they are, they have powers of oppressing body and mind.

On the night of Kim's disappearance the raiders returned. Hordes in brown shirts and swastika armbands. Once again I smelled their sweaty bodies, saw them storm through my parents' house — knives slashing the upholstery of French Empire chairs, boots trampling priceless Meissen china. Fine oriental carpets, thrown into the looters' van. Paintings torn from the walls. Faded squares in the dining room, where Canaletto's London painting had hung; in the morning room, where we'd lived in the rural serenity of paintings by Ruysdael and Constable, Spitzweg and Van de Velde. Empty walls in father's library; gone the grace and gaiety of Degas' horses and Teniers' country people.

All at once a shifting of images. Water. High waves rising, breaking, battering the children. Jimmy in American army uniform, running to help. Quentin and Rose lifted on the crests, falling, deluged, drowning.

'Be careful', my father was pleading with the Nazi with the gun in his hand. 'Your men mustn't damage the paintings; tell them . . .' The gun cracking down on my father's hand. The terrible sound of breaking bones.

Pains in my hand. A slow awakening. Night. An English gale punishing an old English village. Not acts of man; an act of God. I grappled back into consciousness, the horror still tightening my throat. Feeling sick. Feeling the guilt of not having shared my parents' last journey. Words to exorcise the nightmares. 'My hand hurts.' Blessed English words, 'My hand hurts. All right, I won't be a fool. My bones are whole. It's psychosomatic and I know all about it. And when one knows what it is one can deal with it.' Gruber barking? Wake up and think; it's Kim who's missing.

The sky was getting lighter, shapes of racing clouds visible above the black contours of the Downs. The wind was still strong. But there was something else, the voice of a thrush calling the morning. The overture filled out with the rising song of blackbirds and finches, wagtails and tits and sparrows; even a cuckoo.

As I listened to the dawn chorus, pitting itself against the storm, I suddenly heard a new sound.

I ran downstairs. No doubt. It had to be Kim's front paws belabouring the door.

He limped in, head drooping, soaking wet, and collapsed on the kitchen floor.

I held him, wrapped in our softest bath towel, while Alex examined him. Kim didn't mind; he was fast asleep.

'His paws are a bit sore,' said Alex. 'Can't see any real damage. He's exhausted, that's all.'

'What can I do?' Kim, with his coat wet and plastered down, looked so tiny and frail.

'You can stop worrying about the little beast. Put him in his basket and let him sleep it off . . . whatever it is he needs to sleep off.'

For a couple of days and nights Kimmy left his basket only to empty his bladder and bowels and to eat and drink. He slept and slept, dead to the life around him, oblivious to Sooty's efforts at worrying him out of his sluggishness.

On the third day after the great escape Sooty, unable to paw Kim from his bed, plonked herself on top of him. At last Kim raised his head. He gazed at the fluffy tail, draped over his face, took it between his teeth, and sent Sooty leaping off his basket. He followed her, stretched, yawned and sniffed the scent of boiling meat.

Rising on his hindlegs he gave me his usual salute. Then, together with Sooty, he went to inspect the cottage from top to bottom. The two of them criss-crossed our garden, made for the hole in the hedge and went on to check Kim's second domain next door.

'Our boy is back on his feet!' Renée called over the hedge. 'My God! What a dog!' She laughed. 'Who'd have thought it of him? Eileen's told me all about it.'

'Eileen?'

'Your friend who owns the little dachs bitch.'

'Renée, what has she told you?'

'Well, about Kimmy turning up that evening.'

'You mean at Plumpton?'

'Hasn't she told you?'

'No.'

'I expect she'll phone you.'

'She might have phone me when she found Kim.'

'Well, you know her. She's rather casual. So you don't know the story?'

'I'd like to hear it.'

'Our Sir Timothy went to visit Lottie. Eileen thinks he got into the house through the cat-door. Anyway, she found him with Lottie, asleep in her basket. Eileen meant to give him something to eat. But when he wakened up he went straight to the door. She let him out . . . she thought he wanted to spend a penny . . . and off he went. My God! What a walk for a little one! Fourteen miles at least.'

Yes; seven miles there, on a terrible night, and seven miles home. How had he found the way? On his two previous visits to Lottie's house we'd gone there by car.

Renée and I watched Kim enjoy his new-found energy. Sooty, on the branch of an apple tree, was provocatively swishing her tail while Kim, on his hindlegs, was working up to a mighty leap. As usual he failed in emulating the cat and finished head over heels on the lawn.

Renée said, 'I hope his journey hasn't been wasted.'

At the proper time, exactly sixty-three days after

Kimmy's expedition, we heard the results; three puppies, one red, two black and tan.

Miss Joy, looking at Kim with an expert's eye, had to admit that he wasn't a runt after all. His shoulders were not too loose, ears and tail were well feathered and his coat had become full and glossy. But Miss Joy predicted trouble; Kim's love affair with Lottie was regrettable because it would unsettle the dog. He'd miss his mate and become a roamer.

Richard, in his schoolboy wisdom, suggested a method of forestalling such escape-impulses. There was no better cure for restlessness than sports. And so he presented Kim with a full-sized black and white football as used by television-conscious cup final teams.

In relation to the dog the ball was very large indeed, and Kim's first reaction was to run away from it. But as the ball didn't pursue him he changed his tactics. He stalked it, as Sooty had taught him, and pounced. The ball, annoyingly, shot away from him. He followed it, slowly and thoughtfully, rose on his hindlegs and grabbed hold of it with his powerful front paws.

Richard told him that it was against soccer rules to take the ball in one's hands, but Kim had other ideas. He clearly thought that the ball was meant to be destroyed. Clinging to it, he began to lick it. The thing was to make it soft. After a good deal of hard tongue-work Kim bared his teeth and took a bite. But the ball was too big and his mouth bounced off. Kim wouldn't admit failure. Gripping hard, shoulder muscles straining, he looked like a miniature bull and with the stubbornness of a bull he kept attacking the maddening object.

Patiently Richard repeated a demonstration of how to dribble a ball. Kim watched. Eventually, nose and shoulders nudging the ball, he gave a good imitation of Richard's technique. He dribbled the ball into the box Richard had set down as a goal. But having made such a concession he again mounted the ball and reverted to his own lick-and-bite method.

Whether it was the energetic ball-work or natural contentment, Kim proved Miss Joy wrong. He did not go roaming. On the contrary, he let us know that he much preferred walking on the lead to being let loose on the cricket field where he might be embarrassed by forward and frisky bitches.

One day, after a vigorous ball game, Kim came into my study and crept under the couch. For many months he'd done no such thing; he'd leaped *on* the couch. He seemed dejected; and after a while he began to cry, very softly and miserably.

Of course I went down on the floor. 'What's the matter boy? Thorn in your paw? Let me see.'

Kim let me check his feet, his joints and back. There was no detectable injury, yet he was still moaning.

'What is it?' His nose was hot and dry.

Suddenly Kim put a front paw on my hand, held it down and then, in no uncertain manner, put his head into my palm.

I pushed back his lips. 'So that's it.' Sure enough, his bottom teeth looked rotten.

While I'd examined his mouth Kim had stopped crying, but the moment I withdrew my hands he complained again.

I phoned Alex. 'Kim's got toothache. Could you come home and take him to the vet?'

'Look, I'm busy. You take him.'

'I can't.'

'Why?'

'Because I can't drive and hold his head at the same time.'

'What!'

'The dog's in pain. The only thing that stops him crying's my keeping his head in my hands.'

'All right, I'll come.'

Within the hour we were in the surgery of Miss Joy's vet. 'That's the trouble with dachsies,' he told us, 'Their teeth tend to go rotten at a young age. Afraid I'll have to take out most of his bottom teeth . . . Don't worry, it won't hurt. We'll give him a general anaesthetic. You can fetch him around six.'

I handed Kim over. What else could I do? 'Back soon,' I said to the dog. He'd been content with that promise whenever I'd had to leave him at home.

Alex had to go back to the hospital. I wandered aimlessly around Brighton, haunted by the accusation in Kimmy's eyes. He hadn't believed me. He'd understood all too well that he'd been delivered into the hands of a stranger for some sinister purpose. He was in pain, and I had abandoned him.

Wishing away time, I walked along the seafront. I drifted into a cinema, walked out half way through the movie, returned to the surgery much too early and hung around the empty waiting room.

When the vet arrived at last he looked reassuringly placid. 'Kim's been no trouble . . . Let's get him.' He took me to a back room and opened a small cage. 'Here we are.' He put the limp dog into my arms. 'I expect he'll be dopey for the next twenty four hours. Just let him sleep. If he wants food let him have the usual. His lower jaw will hang open for a week or two, so he'll dribble. But that'll stop once his gums have hardened.'

Kim didn't stay dopey for long. On the drive home he opened his eyes and acknowledged our presence with lively tailwagging. At the cottage he jumped out of the car and jostled us to the kitchen.

'Milk?'

Obviously. He made excited little sounds in his throat, his normal expression of pleasure.

We watched Sir Timothy make a meal of milk, brown bread and meat. And for days after we watched him for possible side-effects of his operation or the anaesthetic. At the very least we expected that his jaw would hang open.

But Kim never dribbled. He kept his mouth clamped shut. It gave him a look of uncanny determination. As Alex put it, Kim was keeping a stiff lower lip.

Our dachs had become a very stoical and positive

Kim keeping a stiff lower lip

character. It was just as well. Before long he needed his courage and self-assurance.

CHAPTER TEN

Ever since we'd acquired Paul I had persuaded myself that children and animals are no trouble. Well, perhaps no trouble; but they certainly make demands on one's time. The better they like living with one, the more time-consuming they are.

There were moments when I hated being interrupted in the middle of writing a crucial chapter of a book. Yet I came to realize that it was a measure of success when Paul, who had so many friends of his own age, settled down in my study for a long talk or asked me to go hiking with him. And Sir Timothy also liked all the attention he could get. He'd bump the door until it would spring open, push it wider with his nose, come and put a paw on my knee and wait to be talked to. 'Good dog, go away,' wouldn't do. He still wanted to hear stories and he'd comment on them with small noises which were as expressive as human language.

A time came when I had to short-change Kim because my chores for people increased.

As I'd feared, Vicky's husband had finally left her. Alex and I had agreed to look after the children, Quentin and Rose, until she'd settled her affairs in Canada. I'd also undertaken to find a flat in London for her. About the same time the Bocks, in California, accepted our offer to take over Jimmy for his final school year.

We obviously needed a larger house. As it happened, a truly spacious one was coming up for auction. The oldest part of it dated back to the fifteenth century, the *new* wing was Georgian. There were flint-walled outhouses, fine lawns, an enormous open terrace and a walled orchard.

There were also considerable snags, which Kim and I discovered in the course of a long afternoon.

Probes with my pocket knife revealed areas of dry rot, wet rot, woodworm and deathwatch beatle damage. The

ique and inadequate. The electric wiring
rtainly in a dangerous state. As to the
re were no less than sixteen pipes, as far as I
stly obsolete, draped all over the kitchen. And
g-masterpiece was a toilet planted in front of a
la ow with its tank fixed to the window frame. Besides, the house needed decorating inside and outside, and the front of it was too near a main road. We'd have to forget the Georgian front and use the safe side door.

Kim also had reservations. He did not care for the long flights of stairs and he found the cellars rather wet underfoot. He also suspected that the place was haunted and bravely growled at a variety of creaking and gurgling sounds. I told him that the house would be lovely after we'd re-constructed it. Despite all the snags it was meant for a dog and a family of children.

When Alex went over the place in the evening he also pointed out its nearness to the road. But he noticed that the sounds of traffic did not penetrate; the walls were two feet thick. What attracted him most was the gardens; an ancient figtree growing against the south wall, a fine yew hedge, old-fashioned scented roses and a thicket of bulbs and flowering shrubs.

Indoors he discovered even more snags than I and he was not impressed when I pointed out the beautiful proportions of the rooms.

He said, 'The surveyors' report's bound to be terrible.'

'That's right,' I agreed. 'Let's not bother with surveyors.'

'What!'

'Why pay for a report advising you not to buy the house? The basics are all right; the walls are good enough for a fortress and the roof's wavey but sound.'

'Oh yes?' Alex took me by the arm and marched me back to the attic. 'Give me your penknife.'

He climbed up the loft-ladder and jabbed the knife into one of the great oak-timbers. Half the blade disappeared into a maze of worm-holes and channels. Fine dust came powdering down.

'Won't the knife go any deeper?' I asked.

'No.'

'Try somewhere else.'

Alex made tests all over the attic. Finally, getting fed up with the pests, he jabbed even harder. The blade of the knife snapped. He laughed. 'All right. You win. It would take the woodworm and deathwatch beetles of the whole village several centuries to destroy these timbers. Underneath they're as hard as rock . . . But we'll have to get rid of the rot and the active pests, and that'll be an expensive business.'

'Not if I do the job. A firm would charge at least fifteen hundred pounds to treat the exposed timbers . . . I've seen the small print on this type of contract. The firms take no responsibility for the wood inside walls.'

'Because they can't be got at.'

'The worm penetrates by making channels. Right? If one gets the Rentokil liquid to run into those channels one can clean up the wood all the way through . . . All I need is your discarded hypodermic syringes.'

For once Alex did not say that it wouldn't work. He just looked at the great roof and the attics and shook his head. 'It's a task for a Hercules.'

'Or for a very small woman who can easily get in and out of the rafters.'

'And the cellars?'

'Same treatment.'

'You'll knock yourself out.'

'Less than by working on a typewriter six hours at a stretch.'

'The attics could be quite useful,' said Alex.

'If we take the central heating and the lighting all the way up. Plenty of room for Paul's photographic work.'

'It won't be easy to get a billiard table up here.'

'We can start with table tennis. Quentin and Rose play well.'

'Madelaine, you'd better start with a visit to our bank manager.'

Alex's work did not allow him to take time off. It was I who had to convince our bank manager that something could be made of the old house, who had to tell the estate agent that we were well aware of the poor state it was in, and who had to go to the auction.

Never having attended an auction it seemed madness, even to me, that my first experience should entail my bidding thousands of pounds. What if I was too slow in raising my hand? What if a fly came to sit on my nose and made me raise a hand at the wrong time? Clutching Kimmy, I worked out what seemed a reasonable policy. I'd keep absolutely still, hands on the dog, until the last bid. Then, a fraction of a second before the auctioneer's hammer would come down, I'd make my one and only bid in a loud, clear voice.

I had the impression that the four people bidding for *our* house had done this sort of thing before. There was such nonchalance in the way they raised their brochures. While I was trembling with tension, they looked almost bored. Didn't they care whether or not they won the contest for the property. Did they have so much money that it didn't matter how much they paid for it? The seconds between each bid seemed to last hours.

At last, silence. At last the auctioneer's hammer rose. 'Going, going . . .'

My arm shot up. I'd lost my voice.

The auctioneer had seen me. Fortunately. Down came the hammer, quite inevitably, and the auctioneer calmly announced that the house was sold to the lady with the dog.

I went home in a state of euphoria. I was about to call Alex, to let him know that I'd purchased the house at our price, when the telephone rang.

The auctioneer was on the line. 'Would you like to make a fast buck?' He was laughing. 'We have a client who wants the house you've just bought. A doctor. He was going to attend the auction but — just as he was leaving his surgery — a woman brought him a baby who'd swallowed a button. So he didn't make it . . . If you let him have the house he'll give you a cheque for a thousand pounds. You see, a fast buck. If I were you, I'd take it.'

'If you were me, you wouldn't.'

'You'll have to do an awful lot to the house before you can live in it.'

'I know.'

'Whatever will you do with a place that size?'

'Fill it with children.'

'Well, well.' Again the jovial chuckle. 'You'll have to get yourselves a bigger dog to guard the property.'

'Sir Timothy Hemjoy will manage perfectly well.'

'Sir . . . who?'

The story spread with true village-speed. We were starting a school at the big house. We were starting a nursing home for children. We had Home Office permission to make the house into a borstal institution for first offenders.

Alex and I enjoyed the rumours and added to them. We let it be known that we hadn't yet decided whether to run the place as a kennels, a nursery, a gaming club or a discotheque.

Some people, like the screamers, were displeased. It had taken them years to decide our status as professional people suitably housed in a modest cottage. They were afraid they might have to revise their attitudes. What were they to make of us in an immodestly large house? Were we to be treated as tradesmen (a discotheque!), thus losing status, or as 'county'? The difficulty of moving us up to county was that our professions were wrong for that status. It was a great problem to all but us and our real friends.

Renée, always warm and generous, laughingly added to the confusion by telling the village snobs that she and Richard had compelled us to leave the cottage because of their noisiness.

When we decided to rename the house the fat really was in the fire. Removing a totally unhistorical name, we re-christened it Romaine House — because Alex and I had met in Rome and because the boundary of the garden was an old Roman road. The parochial London commuters who lived in the village reproved us; and a member of the Preservation Society, also a commuter, wrote us quite an offensive letter.

But, on the whole, the village simmered down faster than we'd expected. Spite and speculation gave way to simple curiosity and even approval. As squads of builders and craftsmen began to resurrect the hidden beauties of Romaine House, more and more people began to enjoy the improvements which — after all — enhanced the charms of the whole village.

While I worked alongside the men, treating the wormeaten timbers, Kimmy — getting little attention — laboured at turning himself into an efficient guard dog. Covering large rooms, long passages and stairways, he taught himself to discriminate between those who did jobs of work and those who had no business in the house. I soon learned to pay attention to Kim's barking because he always barked for a good reason — at suspect strangers and unknown motorists who used our garage-approach for turning their cars.

Undemandingly Kim worked with me at Romaine House, accompanied me when I went apartment hunting for Vicky and went with me to schools where I sought places for Quentin, Rose and Jimmy. The only time the little dog made himself felt was late in the evening. When I sat down at the end of a day, with a book or some sewing, he'd jump on my lap — a thing he'd rarely done before life became so hectic. No matter what was in my hands, he'd wriggle under books and building plans and stake a claim even beneath curtain-materials full of pins.

We moved into Romaine House less than a week before the children were due to arrive. Everything functioned; plumbing, heating, telephone, lights. The rooms looked as lovely as I'd imagined them on my first visit to the house.

But something was missing. The house was as light and spacious as my childhood home in Neustadt, yet there was something sad about the great expanses of naked wall. As we wandered through our new home I missed, as never before, the paintings I'd grown up with — the landscapes of Constable and Ruysdael, the peopled canvases of Teniers, the Russian scenes of Vereschagin and Winogradow, the dancers and horses of Degas.

Our only picture, Miss Ethel's Sussex landscape, looked very small and lost.

Kathy and I were sorting out the china, which the removal men had stacked on the dining room table, when I thought I heard footsteps across the hall. We listened. All was quiet.

'If you had visitors Kim would let us know,' said Kathy. 'All the same, perhaps we should lock some of the doors.' There were two sets of french windows in the lounge, and three other outside doors. 'We've got used to leaving everything open . . . I mean, it was all right in the cottage, with neighbours all around us. But here we're more secluded . . . Things aren't what they used to be. We've had a burglary in my sister-in-law's road; and that's council houses. They took the television and an electric kettle.'

'Listen!'

This time we both heard it; stealthy footsteps. And still Kim wasn't barking.

Silently, we made our way into the hall and entered the lounge by a door on the far side. That way we could overlook the forty-foot room without being seen by intruders.

There were two of them, hard at work and talking quietly. I motioned Kathy to keep still.

'Mais non Richard,' Renée was saying. *'L'autre; la rose rouge.'* She was on her knees before our inglenook fireplace. In it she had placed an enormous, very beautiful, barrel-shaped vase which she was filling with flowers. The bare recess was being transformed, starkness at once stressed and mellowed. *'La même rose,* Richard.'

He was handing her another spray of dark red Frensham. Kim, jealous of the attention she was lavishing on the flower-arrangement, went on his back, paws up, and wriggled flirtatiously.

'Le pauvre petit,' Renée patted his belly. *'Il travaille quoiqu'il soit las.'*

'Mum, don't speak French to the dog. You'll confuse him.'

'Confuse Kim! He already understands more French than you do. And Paul's Viennese too. Unlike you, he doesn't need a dictionary.'

'Well, I reckon he does. Kim's proper language is English.'

'How do you know?'

'Really mum! Don't you ever listen to dogs? The difference couldn't be more obvious, especially when we're in Switzerland. It's clear; German dogs bark in German . . . sort of *kroff-kroff- kraut-kroff.* And French dogs sound French *Cha-grin cha-grin choucroute chagrin.'*

'Richard! My God!'

'Ssht . . . mum, do be quiet. You'll get us caught.'

Renée sat back on her heels, surveying her flower arrangement. 'It's not one of my best, is it?'

'Don't be silly, mum. It's great. Come on, let's go.'

I walked in on them. 'Richard's right; dogs do bark in their native languages. In Spain it's *oiga hijo oiga hijo.'*

'Oh!' Renée had turned, 'I told Richard he was making too much noise. Now . . .'

'Really mum! Who told whom? Madelaine, we wanted it to be a surprise.'

'It is. It's lovely.'

'I had this vase in the loft,' said Renée. 'It's much too large for our cottage . . . we had an idea it would look nice in your fireplace . . .'

'Mum thought your lounge looked sort of bare . . .'

'Richard!' A gust of laughter. 'Richard! My God!'

They kept coming. Mona Kilpack — tall, handsome, talented — with a painting that celebrated a Brighton spring. 'Thought this might look right in your new house. I've got picture cord and hooks. I'll hang it for you.'

Dr Bogey; 'What you need in your dining room is this.'

This was a beautiful watercolour of a sunlit pond by Charles Knight R.A. 'And . . .' rather shyly, 'I don't know whether you care for this sort of thing . . .' One of the doctor's own calligraphy panels, already framed, KNOWLEDGE AND VIRTUE AND A HORSE'S MOUTH SHOULD NOT PASS THROUGH TOO MANY HANDS.

Ginette Bruce-Lockhart — French, volatile painter of dreams — with a surrealist painting of a minute crucifix and two little nuns dominated by a huge robot. 'I thought something that links the past and the future would fit this house . . . I call it *the juggernaut.*' Was I permitted to call it *alas poor spirit?* 'Why not? it's yours.'

Jane Williams. When she'd been an art student she'd run out of models and I had sat for her. 'You probably don't remember me . . . I did some portraits of you. I always meant to give you one. In a big house like this you might want some paintings.'

A sunlit pond, by Charles Knight R.A.

Most unexpected of all; a stranger. 'You don't know me, by my husband and I feel that we've known you for a long time. Your books have given us so much pleasure . . .

we always wanted to say *thank you*. Suddenly I got an idea how we could do it . . . I saw you in the village with you little dog . . . But if you don't like them I'll think of something else.'

Them were a pair of early Victorian watercolour pictures of red long-haired dachshunds, lovingly and meticulously painted by a Miss Mercy Creed. The dog of the pair was a perfect portrait of Gruber.

The portrait by Jane Williams

On the eve of the children's arrival from Canada we were hanging the last pair of curtains and half watching a much exhibited television interviewer interview another much exhibited interviewer. All twitches and stern godlikeness, they were pontificating on *our era,* rolling off platitude after platitude as if they were pearls of profundity. Clearly Sex, like last year's beauty queen, had become unfashionable and the in-thing of the mass media was to be Violence. The interviewers were plugging the in-thing very smoothly. '. . . I mean, we absolutely agree . . . I mean all intelligent people are well aware that our society is absolutely depraved and brutal . . .'

I didn't have to be reminded. I wasn't likely to forget my first-hand experiences of depraved and brutal people. Were they as many as five per cent of the human race? But what a pity the other ninety-five per cent were not worth mentioning — certainly not on the media — because they were the undramatic ones who love and grow flowers, care about one another and paint pictures. It was they who had given meaning to our new home. Their works were all around us.

Suddenly the chit-chat on the box was drowned by the telephone. In the big lounge it sounded as loud as a fire engine bell.

'How's your doggie?' enquired the voice of our telephone operator.

'Fine, thanks.'

'He doesn't mind all them stairs in the new house?'

'He's getting used to them.'

'Like I said . . . strays from the R.S.P.C.A. are all right, but you can't beat a properly bred pup . . . I had an auntie . . .'

'You must be tired,' I suggested. 'It's rather late . . .'

'Oh, I was never one to mind the work. Talk! sometimes I went on talking till I was fit to drop. It's all been part of the service, taking an interest in my regulars.'

'You're very helpful, I know . . .'

'That's all over. As of now you're fully automatic.'

'Me . . . automatic?' Ginette's robot, bestriding Christ

and the little nuns, seemed to come stalking out of its frame 'Automatic? Not me!'

'Nothing you can do about it, dear,' said the operator. 'As of now I'm going off the air; you'll have to *dial* the numbers you want. The service won't be what it used to be . . . you mark my word . . . Anyway, I just called to say good-bye.'

'Good-bye, and thank you for all your help.'

'Sorry about the service. With all them electronics it just won't be efficient any more. Well . . . love to the doggie. Bye-bye . . . Oh! hang on! I'm not meself tonight. I nearly forgot. You having friends from Canada staying with you?'

'They're arriving tomorrow.'

'Relations?'

'Yes . . . first cousins twice removed. A red Indian chief and his squaw.'

'Go on! well . . . I mean, I know you're sort of foreign. You write books, don't you? A red Indian! Fancy that . . . Well, I don't know what's come over me; I nearly forgot . . . there's a telegram for your red Indians.'

The telegram from Canada was from John, the father of Quentin and Rose. *Welcome home darlings,* he'd cabled, *all my love, Daddy.*

The yellow envelope stayed in my handbag. What would the children make of it? If their father loved them so much, why had he left them and their mother and gone to the other end of Canada? As to being welcomed home, could there be a home for them without their parents? It seemed so, yet we distrusted the ease with which they settled down.

Of course life had been exciting for them; the journey on the ship, re-discovering Sussex, exploring a new house and gardens, the meeting with people they'd known all their lives. And there was Kim. Never having owned a dog, they found him quite absorbing.

Kim was equally interested in Quentin and Rose, partly because he liked to be well acquainted with anyone who came into the household, partly because — as a good guard dog — he didn't believe in trusting newcomers too quickly. Kim was none too fond of our untidy, overgrown vegetable garden, yet he'd follow the children and watch attentively while they picked sweet corn for dinner. And he'd follow at their heels until the basket was handed over to me in the kitchen.

The early autumn evenings were so mild that we could eat out in the open, at the big stone table on the terrace. The children enjoyed the scent of roses, the beautiful sunsets and the candlelit dusk.

'I love the things that Alex grows,' declared Rose, a few days after she and Quentin had arrived. 'Especially the corn.' She sank her teeth into her fifth or sixth cob.

'We had corn in Canada,' Quentin reminded her.

'It wasn't as tender.'

Quentin studied the dishes in front of him, the laden baskets of apples and plums from the orchard. 'I hope mother is eating . . . She promised she would, but I don't trust her. When father left us she sort of stopped eating properly.' Quentin suddenly looked much more than his ten years. 'It was difficult . . . When I cooked something for mum, she'd have it all right. But I couldn't always do it . . . I had to leave her and go to school.'

Quite unreasonably, I felt angry with Vicky. How could she have put the burden of her unhappiness on this little boy! I was no longer reluctant to admit to myself that my friend Vicky was not an admirable character, that she'd always been extremely selfish. As to her meanness and avariciousness, none but her husband could surpass it. It was sad. I'd watched Vicky become more and more obsessed with money grabbing; I'd seen John turn from a poor young well-to-do student into an academic with an eye on the main chance. Quentin and Rose had grown up in an atmosphere of a false, lofty intellectualism and private meanness. Their parents' images of one another had also been false and when they'd discovered the truth about each other the marriage had broken down.

Quentin said, 'Mum's got so thin.'

'She's always been thin.' Rose helped herself to another

apple. 'I wonder when daddy's going to write to us.'

Alex looked at me. He was right, of course. I couldn't keep back the telegram indefinitely. I took it out of my bag and gave it to Rose. 'I think he has written.'

She opened the envelope avidly. 'Quentin, it is from dad. I told you he wouldn't forget.' She read the cable and passed it across to her brother.

Quentin picked it up, held it for a moment and then threw it aside — unread. 'I am not interested.'

The gesture was so adult, so painfully final, that even Rose had to accept it. She sat in silence, head bowed, the half eaten apple drooping from her hand.

'Mao-tse-tung!' called a voice from the footpath beyond the garden. 'Mao-tse-Tung! Where are you? Kitty-kitty-kitty!'

The children turned. And there, by the terrace door, sat Kim. He'd turned his back on a very large marmalade cat which looked all set for a fight. Part of Kim's self-imposed policing duties consisted of chasing strange cats out of his territory; it was something we'd witnessed almost every day. Yet now, he grimly refused to acknowledge the presence of a cat. Tail quivering, he sat tight. He was obviously aware of the intruder, yet the stubbonness of his pose made it very clear that he was not going to submit to the indignity of fighting a cat so much larger than himself.

Quentin's frown gave way to a warm smile. 'Kim, you clever, clever dog.' He left the table and scooped our dachs into his arms. Mao-tse-Tung was pussy-footing off the terrace. 'That's the thing to do with big beasts; ignore them. Here, you can have a bit of cheese. You deserve it . . . Thank God for dogs!'

Kimmy hated trains as much as he loved cars. All the same, I decided to take him on one train journey to London; because the children wanted him to come, but chiefly because Paul was leaving the country that day.

We'd never doubted that Paul would carry out his intention of becoming a graphic artist and printer. We'd known that he was reading the relevant journals of several

PAUL, independent at eighteen

countries and applying for scholarships. And yet, when Paul's passport to the future had arrived it had seemed unexpected — that letter offering him a work and study contract with an international company. The terms were exceptional; a free apartment, a salary, free education at the Technical University in Vienna, part time work with the firm and finally management training. Our decisive schoolboy had turned into an equally positive adult who, at eighteen, had achieved independence.

Paul's portrait of hisson, young Alex

But Paul was not too grown up to show his pleasure when I told him that Kim would see him off at the air terminal.

On the way to town the dog stayed buttoned up inside his coat. At Victoria station, disgusted with the clanging of trains and trolleys, he pulled hard to get out into the street, but the engine of the taxi pacified him and he went to sleep. Kim didn't like the air terminal because he detested luggage. Suitcases meant that one of his people was going away. Paul's departure depressed him, but he cut his losses and perked up when he realized that Quentin, Rose and I were staying with him.

We had a full day. Quentin and Rose, who'd temporarily attended a school near us, went to be interviewed at a school to which they'd transfer upon the return of their mother. We inspected the flat I'd found for Vicky and the children, bought pots and pans, ordered a cooker, arranged for the installation of the telephone, and visited Vicky's future landlords. The kindly family, who had remodelled their Victorian house to make the new flat, gave us a big tea.

By the time we got to the nearest subway station it was the evening rush hour. Though I kept Kimmy under my arm he obviously found the great crowd on the platform bewildering. He kept turning his head, eyes wide, trying to keep track of the people milling around us.

The first train that came in was wrong for us. But the sheer pressure of bodies was such that I was separated from the children and almost pushed through the gaping doors. I tried to stay put but some of the travellers were hemming me in.

Suddenly Kim began to snarl and growl. The man next to me, startled and scared, shrank away and I managed to get clear of the scrum. The train pulled out.

On the near-empty platform Kim and I rejoined the children. And when our train arrived there was no crush. We even found seats.

I was going to light a cigarette when I notice that the flap of my handbag was turned back. Even before looking inside I knew that someone had deliberately opened it. None but Kim had been aware of the mugging. He'd done his best to stop the thief and — almost certainly — saved the greater part of the objects inside my bag.

What had gone was my pocket diary and my wallet, containing driving licence, car insurance certificate, my membership cards of various clubs and societies, bank-card, our train tickets and money.

The children and I scraped together our loose change, not even enough for the fare home.

CHAPTER ELEVEN

The mugging in the subway troubled me, though not for the obvious reasons. It raised uncomfortable questions in my mind. Was violence sharply increasing, even in our relatively law-abiding country? I'd believed that the emphasis on crime and violence had become the in-thing of the media. Was it the other way about? Was it the real world which was dictating the keynote of the mass media? Was I being foolish in thinking that there was less evil now than in the Hitler period of my childhood?

I was more disturbed by the fact that I'd been robbed than by my actual losses. Apart from the emotional shock the worst loss was, oddly enough, my pocket diary. In it I'd recorded dates and forward engagements a year ahead, lectures to societies and universities, publishing schedules, the arrivals and departures of friends. But the one arrival I hadn't forgotten was Jimmy's.

Alex and I left early in the morning, by car. On the way to London airport we talked of Jimmy as we remembered him. Four years earlier Jimmy Bock had accompanied us on a trip to Italy. He'd been an easy-going thirteen year old with a strong sense of humour. What would he be like at seventeen? A hippie, Alex maintained.

After the plane from California had touched down I wondered whether I'd even recognize the boy. But I needn't have worried. He emerged from the customs hall looking like an American father's idea of an English-style young man; drip-dry grey suit, collar and tie, blond hair almost shorn.

His face hadn't changed much, except that it looked moody and unsmiling. But the rest of him had grown enormous. He was about six foot six tall and as broad as a baseball player.

He greeted us with a mumbled 'hi', let Alex carry his luggage, shambled to the car with us and filled the back seat. After taking off his tie, shoes and socks he went fast asleep. Big and strong as Jimmy was, the journey from California had just about knocked him out.

At home, he walked into the house, unseeing and incurious. No, he didn't want anything to eat. He was just gonna rest. Did he want to be called for dinner. Dinner? The evening meal. Oh no, he didn't care for sit-down meals; he just ate when he felt like it.

We lugged Jimmy and his suitcases upstairs. He threw himself on the bed and went back to sleep.

'You won't find him as angelic as he used to be,' said Alex.

'The poor boy's tired.'

'I wonder what he'll be like when he isn't.'

So did I. What next? Somehow Jimmy had made me feel very unsure of the school arrangements I'd made for him. Meanwhile there was nothing I could do for him and I went to open my mail.

There was a letter from a London Lost Property Office, telling me that my wallet had been handed in. There was a letter enclosing the bank card I'd lost and another, from the London police, telling me that someone had handed in my driving licence.

Suddenly I felt good, completely happy, equal to getting along with a dozen hippies. So much for this evil world. One thief had stolen from my handbag; but three separate people had picked up the pieces the thief had thrown away. In the middle of the rush hour they'd taken the trouble to help a stranger. And they'd gone out of their way to return what the thief had discarded. Only one of those people had given his name and address — because the police had asked him for it.

Somehow the proofs of human decency I'd received lessened my apprehensions about Jimmy. Clearly, like many of his young fellow Americans, he was in revolt against the world around him and frustrated about his present inability to change society. There was little I could do about that, but I'd try to give him some confidence in simple human values — in those qualities that survive concentration camps and wars.

When he emerged from his room, twenty-four hours later, he'd showered and changed into jeans and an undershirt.

While he was eating a plate of bacon and eggs Kim at last had his chance of exploring the newcomer. He sniffed Jim's bare feet, decided they were clean, and gave them a lick.

'Gee!' Jim looked almost scared. 'Is this a dawg? He's so little; if I step on him I'll kill him.'

'Don't worry,' I told him. 'Kim's good at avoiding feet.'

Kim was having a hard time surveying Jimmy. He sat, head lifted skyward, trying to see Jim's face. It was too high up. He then jumped on a chair and mounted the table. I chased him off. Kim prowled about the room, trying to find a spot which would afford him a total view of our guest. Still no good. Jimmy was the biggest person the dog had ever tried to deal with. Finally, as Jim rose from the table, Kimmy followed him on his hind legs. Jimmy very nearly smiled but chose to ignore the dog. Kim sulkily retired to his basket.

'What do I do now?' asked Jim, forlornly.

'We're going to Brighton to buy your clothes.' Even as I said it the very idea of that young giant in school uniform seemed ridiculous.

Jimmy, still sleepy, submitted to wearing shoes, to the car journey and to the crowded shops. At the school outfitters he suffered himself to be squeezed into grey suits which were much too tight.

The obviously experienced shop assistant was becoming exasperated. 'If I may say so, modom, even our biggest size is not quite . . . Modom, schoolboys just don't come this size.'

'They do, from America. You'll just have to make the suits to measure.'

It was the same story with the regulation shoes. Size twelve had to be ordered specially.

'Do I have to wear shoes at all?' asked Jimmy.

'I'm afraid so.'

'Madelaine, I hate shoes. Back home I always go barefoot.'

'Sorry Jim.' We were walking past shop after shop full of the kind of clothing he obviously disliked. 'You see, this country isn't warm enough to go barefoot.'

'And the suits we've ordered . . . will I have to wear them all the time?'

'Not at home.'

'Well, I guess they're okay . . . kinda English.' Suddenly Jimmy stopped outside a tobacconists. 'There's something I need,' he muttered and disappeared inside.

I soon discovered what it was. In the car, on the way home, Jimmy produced a pipe. He filled it with tobacco, lit it, and spluttered. 'Guess I'll get used to it . . . It's a real English pipe to go with the school uniform.'

I didn't want to tell him that he wouldn't be allowed to smoke at school. Not yet.

When we got home I fetched my camera and suggested taking a picture of Jimmy with his pipe, for his parents. He consented, but not before taking off his shoes, collar and tie. We went out on the terrace where Kim, once again, tried to get a proper view of Jim.

The dog gave a repeat performance of his earlier efforts; sitting, standing on his hind legs, jumping on a chair and on a table. Then, still frustrated, he tried the last resort. He tipped over on his back, paws up, tail fanned out.

'What a dawg!' Jimmy gave the delightful smile I remembered from his childhood, knelt down and stroked Kim's belly. 'Guess he wants to get in on the act.' He picked Kim up, rose to his full height and clamped the pipe in his teeth. 'Okay Madelaine; I reckon me with such a little dawg looks kinda stoopid. But shoot.'

That evening Jimmy again refused to sit down and join Alex, Quentin, Rose and me for dinner. No, he didn't like *formal* meals and he'd eat when he felt like it. He slammed out and went to his room, and there he stayed.

Around three in the morning I was awakened by unusual

noises and a chink of light under our door. Was Jimmy feeling sick? I got up, went to his room and quietly opened the door. The bed hadn't been slept in though it had obviously been slept on. Jim wasn't in the room, nor in the adjoining bathroom.

I went downstairs, through the study, to the brightly lit kitchen. And then I heard a conversation between Jimmy and Kim. They were in the larder. Jimmy was contemplating a shelf of canned food while sharing a chunk of cheese with the dog.

'Jimmy!' I had visions of a starved boy and an overfed dachs. 'You should have had dinner.'

'Don't like formal kinda meals.'

'But you're hungry now.'

'Sure.'

'All right. I'll cook you a steak.'

'Right now?'

'Yes.'

He watched me take the meat from the fridge and put it under the grill. 'Listen Madelaine, I guess people my age don't communicate with people your age.'

'No? Mind if I keep you company while you eat.'

'It's your house.' It sounded none too friendly.

But when the steak was ready he didn't reject it, nor a basketful of bread and butter.

'Let me explain about dinner.' I sat down opposite him at the kitchen table. 'We have dinner every night between seven and eight, but it's not a formality. It's not just a time for eating; the idea is that all of us get together and exchange news, talk things over, or argue. It's the one part of the day when we make time for one another.'

'You mean, the two kids turn up for dinner too?'

'Of course.'

'Gee Madelaine! Haven't you heard that there's a generation gap?'

'I've read about it,' I assured him. 'Let's make a deal Jimmy. You join us for dinner every night; the rest of the time you can gap or gape as much as you like.'

'Some deal!' Jimmy burst out laughing. 'I guess you and I will get along okay.'

Though Jimmy soon felt at home with us he found his school-life almost intolerable. It was neither his fault nor the school's. It was just that he came from a country which so prided itself on its freedom that even good schools provided no guidance to the young; and discipline was a dirty word.

For the first time in his life poor Jim was expected to live to a timetable. He was made to attend classes, play games, eat and sleep whether he felt like it or not. He was made to wear collars and ties, socks and shoes. Worst of all, his own personality forced him into the hardest and most discouraging work he'd ever done. The fact that schoolboys much younger than he were better educated in almost every subject aroused his competitive spirit. He wasn't going to be the dumb American in an English public school.

Much against his inclination he got down to studying, even at weekends. Unused to sustained concentration, he found it extremely tough. And we found it hard to coax him out of his dejections. His only pleasures were an erratic motorbike he'd acquired and Kimmy's increasing friendship.

Jim could have returned to the States at any time. No one was forcing him to stay for the whole school year. Yet he courageously made up his mind to stick it. Paradoxically his worst moments didn't happen at school but at the American Embassy in London. On his seventeenth birthday he had to go there and register for army service.

On his return from town we took him to a Chinese restaurant for his favourite kind of meal. He didn't appear to enjoy it. Eventually he confessed that he was feeling miserable because he loathed the thought of army service in Vietnam.

'The discipline you'll have to put up with?' I asked.

'I reckon me with such a little dawg looks kinda stoopid. But shoot.'

'You don't understand,' he rebuked me, gently. 'It's that I don't wanna kill guys.'

We discussed ways of becoming a conscientious objector. Jim had heard of one method only, an appeal on religious grounds. But that was not for him, he told us, because in his case it would be a lie.

'But you've given me an idea,' he said. 'I'll write to a friend in California and ask him to find out whether there are other ways of becoming an objector . . . The one thing that won't get me off the hook is the truth. If I told the board that I don't wanna go in the army because I don't wanna hurt or kill people they'd think I'm nuts. They sure wouldn't believe me.'

'The problem may never arise,' Alex pointed out. 'If you go to university . . .'

'Yeah.' Jimmy puffed at his pipe. 'Maybe I'll get in . . . But I don't think I'll be able to stay . . . All that bookwork! I guess I'm not an academic kinda person.'

'You've done very well in geology,' I reminded him.

'Because I like mountains and rocks . . . But working for a degree?'

'Why not? The subject interests you.'

'Well, I guess I have a chance,' he said, without conviction.

At the end of Jimmy's year his father arrived unexpectedly. In his usual whirlwind fashion, Charles announced that he was off to Israel on business. Jimmy and I were to come for the ride. Charles had already bought our tickets. We'd have two days for getting our shots — vaccination, yellow fever, etcetera. I was to drop everything, cancel engagements, forget husband, house and dog. Charles had it figured out. As Quentin and Rose had joined their mother in London, I was fairly free, at least in Alex's opinion. It was he who persuaded me to go.

I'd never even considered a trip to Israel. Yet, suddenly, it was the one country I wanted to visit. My cousin Erika lived in Tel-Aviv, a first cousin I hadn't met since our childhood. She was the only child of my mother's sister and her parents, like mine, had died in concentration camps.

It was a long time since I'd given Erika a thought. Years ago my letters to Israel had remained unanswered. Yet there had been the odd card, announcing her marriage, informing me of the birth of a daughter, requesting a supply of slimming pills.

I sent off a cable announcing my arrival. What did I have to lose? It wouldn't matter if Erika didn't want to know me. If she didn't wish to revive memories of Europe I'd certainly understand. But her answer came; *Welcome, welcome, welcome, look out for the fattest woman at the airport.*

It was not a fat woman I recognized in the crowd at Tel-Aviv but a beautiful face with a small, delicate nose and luminous grey eyes — the face of my mother's family. While Charles and Jimmy went off to their hotel, I found myself engulfed in boisterous warmth.

'Are you hungry? Meet my husband, Max. We're going straight on to a concert. Our daughter is playing the accordion. Her name is Ilit; you remember? She's thirteen. She's wonderful. It's a young people's concert . . . army boys and girls and . . . well, it's like boy scouts and brownies. That's the children. And then we go home and eat. I've made you a gulyash . . . I remember, you like it. And a big Sacher cake. And then we'll talk . . .'

Erika and Max swept me into a great hall. And I tried to take in faces and more faces — in the auditorium, on stage, all around me. Music. Laughter. Acrobatics. Sheer energy. And little Ilit with her big accordion. Ilit, with my mother's and her mother's luminous grey eyes.

It was two in the morning when we arrived at Erika's cool, tiled apartment. She'd prepared a candlelit feast. And while she cajoled me into eating I kept looking at the pictures on her walls. A frame full of family photographs; my parents, hers, our uncles and aunts, our grandparents.

'Do you remember this?' Ilit brought me a little silver-framed picture of Kimmy. 'You sent it to me when I had measles.'

'She keeps Kimmy's photo beside her bed,' said Erika. 'it's her most precious possession.'

Ilit blushed with embarrassment. She and I looked at one another. *Why did parents have to be so tactless? Why did they have to say things about one's most private life? Forgive your mother. It's not easy for grown-ups to remember the climates and feelings of childhood.*

Ilit smiled at me, and kissed her mother's cheek.

As Erika had warned me, we talked. *Do you remember the Russian song your mother sang? Do you know why our grandfather left grandmother? Do you remember the tablecloth Aunt Helen embroidered? Do you know what you mother said to mine? She said Madelaine is like a cabbage; layers and layers, and no two alike. Do you remember that day in the mountains? The wild cyclamen we found, and the scent of them. Do you remember the path beside the canal? And the dead pigeon . . .*

We talked until a rose-red sun lit the roofs of Tel-Aviv. We remembered until the pain drained out of our memories.

The impressions I took home with me were confused. Jimmy and Charles had taken me on so fast a tour of all Israel that I wasn't sure what I had seen or where.

Alex, used to receiving more information from me than he wanted, found my vagueness somewhat surprising. Where was the hospital we'd visited? Where was the Kennedy memorial? I didn't know.

I could only describe a few moments of precious stillness; a desert landscape of sharp-edged sculptured mountains, the blazing colours of Chagall's stained glass windows, seeing the inscription of my parents' names at the shrine of six million concentration camp victims, walking through the ruins of Caesarea above the Mediterranean and recalling the splendours of Rome.

Some sights had seemed new, others strangely familiar. What had taken me completely by surprise had been the old city of Jerusalem. I hadn't been aware that Christianity had any meaning for me and yet — walking the Stations of the Cross — I suddenly understood that I believed in everything Christ had tried to accomplish.

When it came to telling Alex about my Tel-Aviv family I was more coherent. It wasn't difficult to give him a picture of Erika's warmth and vigour, of Max's quiet sense of fun, of Ilit's musical talents and diffident charm.

On the evening Jimmy and his father left for the States we sat in the lounge and did nothing. Alex said he should be cutting the lawns. I knew I should be sewing buttons on his shirts. Instead Alex poured brandies for us and turned on the television news.

A picture came on the screen, a film of a plane dropping bombs on a city. '. . . the first bombs on Tel-Aviv,' said the announcer. 'On the Egyptian front the Israelis . . .'

The telephone rang and I went to answer it.

'A cable for you,' said the voice at the other end. 'I'll read it out . . . *May we send Ilit to you,* stop, *Erika.*'

'The hospital?' asked Alex.

'No . . . It's the war in Israel. Erika's asking us to look after Ilit.'

'Send her a telegram.'

'What shall I say?'

'*Yes,* of course.'

CHAPTER TWELVE

Ilit did not come to us. The Israeli war was over in six days. Erika still didn't write to me, but Ilit did — and in good English. She was so delighted when I sent her pictures of Kimmy that I took to drawing cartoons of him. I don't know how much she wanted to see England, but she talked of meeting Kimmy in every letter.

More than four years passed before she was old enough and free to travel. She wrote that she'd matriculated and passed her driving test and that she had four months' holiday before the next stage in her education. Of course we invited her to stay with us. We received a cable from her, *Kim, at last.*

I was pleased that Ilit was coming and yet apprehensive. Would she miss the company of young people? Our household had become unusually denuded of them. Paul, with his job in Austria, wouldn't be home until the summer. Quentin was at a public school in the north. Rose had gone to a teachers' training college in Wales. Most of our young friends from the village were either at university or, like Richard, working in town. And there was little hope of seeing Jimmy.

Life had not been easy for him. After his return from England he'd hitch-hiked to the Canadian frontier. But the Canadians had not allowed him across because he had no money. He'd turned back to Detroit, worked in a road-gang until he'd saved the required amount and gone into Canada. After a couple of weeks, spent with expatriate Americans, Jimmy had returned to the States and his parents. I believe he'd wanted to prove to himself that he could, if he wanted to, escape further education and army service. He'd had to be sure that he was making a free choice.

Though he succeeded in getting into university he soon became too discouraged to stay. There followed a long

Ilit was coming

battle with armed services boards, army psychiatrists and committees. Jimmy won. He was graded a conscientious objector and put to work in the toughest possible civilian jobs. After two years of hard labour, but with a lot more self-confidence, Jimmy had gone back to university. He was studying geology and this time — he'd written to us — the academic work seemed almost easy. We wouldn't see him again until he'd *made the degree.*

Ilit, it seemed, would be deprived of young people. But there was Kim. As Quentin had said, *thank God for dogs.*

Shortly before Ilit's arrival Alex suggested an evening out. We'd go to a cocktail party at the hospital and afterwards to a French restaurant.

Sir Timothy never had approved of being left alone; he'd always retired to his basket expressing displeasure in every line of his little body. But this time he went berserk. He kept rushing at the gate which separated the orchard from the rest of the garden, barking furiously. He wouldn't go indoors, despite the cold, and in the end I had to carry him in — under protest.

The party at the hospital lasted a couple of hours. Afterwards, much as I like eating out, I didn't want to go on to the restaurant. Neither did Alex. We agreed we weren't hungry, but we knew that it was Kim who'd put us off. His anger at being shut in had been completely out of character.

Kim acknowledged our homecoming with the most perfunctory tailwag and then immediately crept under the couch in my study. The part of the ground floor where he'd been shut in was in a shambles. His basket, in the kitchen, was over-turned, his mattress was in the dining room. His blanket was in the hall where — most unusual for him — he'd made a puddle. And in the study he appeared to have fought a battle with the rugs.

'You delinquent!' Alex scolded. It was our strongest word of disapproval and Kim certainly knew it.

'Perhaps he's unwell . . . What is it Kimmy?'

He remained under the couch. When I winkled him out he was limp and lethargic. There was an unfocused, far-away look in his eyes and his nose felt dry and hot. When Alex inadvertently dropped a coathanger Kim flinched.

'Can a dog have a headache?' I asked Alex.

'It's a funny idea. But I don't see why not.'

'He must have kept on barking, and barked himself into a headache.' Kim weakly wriggled out of my arms and slunk back to his hiding place.

'He's just sulking.'

'I don't think so. Something's worrying him.'

Alex smiled. 'The ghosts, I expect.'

We'd often laughed at Kim when he'd put up his ears at the sound of creaking timbers or air bubbling in the water pipes. When we'd told him it was ghosts he'd usually relaxed and gone about his normal business.

Kimmy stayed under the couch until we went upstairs. Then, as usual, he followed us; but instead of leaping he dragged himself up step by step. He did not, as was his habit, check that we were putting on the bedroom lights and then go down to his basket. Instead he dashed towards the guest wing at the back of the house and barked. And his bark was pitifully hoarse. He'd almost lost his voice.

'He seems quite alert again,' said Alex. 'There can't be much wrong with him.' He watched Kim rush back and forth between our bedroom and the guest bathroom. 'That'll do Kimmy.'

When we were ready for bed Kim still hadn't returned to his own quarters.

'Let him stay with us,' I suggested. 'He's still upset.'

'Oh, all right.'

Kim, just this once permitted to spend the night in our room, curled up by the radiator. But he didn't settle down. He kept wandering around, sniffing the gap under the door, making funny noises. He wouldn't let us sleep.

Yet, in the morning his nose was cold again and he seemed perfectly fit, though still a little depressed. And he would return to the door of the guest bathroom time and again.

Kathy arrived and began her usual household chores in our bedroom. She dusted, cleaned the mirrors and then opened the built-in wardrobe to hoover inside. Suddenly she bent down and picked something off the floor.

'Where does this go?' She handed me a small, empty

leather bag. 'It was on top of your evening shoes.'

I'd last seen it inside the locked wooden box in which I kept my jewellery. It had contained my grandmother's gold Fabergé locket, a piece I hadn't worn for weeks.

The box was no longer locked. It had been forced open. All my jewellery had gone; beautifully made things, hundreds of years old, which had been in my family for generations, and presents from my in-laws, my engagement ring and the brooch Miss Frederica had left me.

I went straight to the guest bathroom. Sure enough, a small window-pane, seven inches by seven, lay shattered on the floor and the window stood open.

I went and called the police.

The Inspector from the Criminal Investigation Department looked at the long list of missing jewels. 'Antiques, nearly all of them. Who'd know that you had them?'

'Millions of people,' I told him, miserably. 'I've been wearing them on television.'

'That's almost advertising them . . . I can't hold out much hope of your getting your jewellery back. If you'd called us last night we might have caught the burglar. Now . . . well, he's had enough time to get your things out of the country. America's a good market for antiques. Pity you didn't pay more attention to your dog.'

'Clever boy.' The other policeman fondled the dog's ears. 'He's certainly told us how the thief did it.'

Now it was obvious. On the evening before, when we'd been about to go to the party, Kim had barked and tried to go from the orchard into the main garden. He'd tried to alert us to a burglar hiding in the dense shrubbery. We should have known better than to carry him indoors and shut him in on the ground floor.

The thief had climbed up a drain pipe, broken the pane in the guest bathroom, opened the latch and let himself in, while Kim — frustrated downstairs — had barked himself hoarse. Afterwards, feeling lousy, the poor dog had done his best to lead us to the point of entry. And we'd laughed at him. All night long Kim had tried to tell us what had happened, and we'd ignored him. How stupid we'd been!

'You've been lucky up to a point,' said the Inspector. 'Seems the burglar made no attempt to take anything on the ground floor. Your dog's saved a fair number of valuables.'

'A little dog like this?'

'Oh, I bet he scared the burglar. By the sound of him Kimmy might be quite large and fierce.'

Sir Timothy Hemjoy, the perfect guard dog. I don't know how the story got around, but we were beseiged by reporters. Kim's picture appeared in the newspapers. Strangers and friends telephoned. And for days after the publicity people stopped us in the street.

'Look! It's Sir Timothy.'

'Look! This is the little dog who fought the burglars.'

'This is the dachsy that had his picture in the papers . . . Isn't he lovely?'

Kim, tail and ears fanned out, thoroughly enjoyed the adulation.

When Kim suddenly became ill we suspected that one of his fans had given him something he shouldn't have eaten. This time it wasn't a passing indisposition such as a headache. The dog was in bad pain. I watched him in the garden, squatting and straining at half-hourly intervals. It seemed he was trying to pass something and it was hurting him. He was crying almost soundlessly, yet like a child in distress. The policemen, who were still calling at our house, worried almost as much as we did.

I took Kim to a veterinary surgeon. The vet diagnosed prostate trouble, prescribed hormone tablets and recommended castration.

Alex said the diagnosis was wrong.

A second vet said the dog probably had an abcess and prescribed a cream.

Alex said this too was rubbish.

Hoping that nature would help, we despairingly watched

Kim suffer. And Ilit was coming, Ilit who'd waited all these years to be with him.

Alex, anxious about hurting the dog even more, would not examine him.

Kim became listless. His coat turned dull. He was so weak that he could no longer go upstairs. He achieved what he'd always wanted — to be allowed to sleep in our bedroom. But at what a price!

Kim should be put down, a third vet told us.

Alex: No one could have handled the dog with greater gentleness

That day Alex went out into the garden and began to clear the dead wood in the shrubbery. Suddenly he came bursting into my study, where Kim lay up against the radiator. He put a bone on my desk, a jagged piece of chicken bone.

'I know what's the matter with the dog,' he said. 'That damned burglar had a meal in the shrubbery . . . I'm going to take a look at Kim's rear end.'

We carried a table into the bathroom and put Kimmy on it. He struggled, weakly, and as I held him he made that heart-breaking soundless noise in his throat. I began to tremble all over. I did believe in Alex's skill. He'd once been awarded a top prize for surgery. No one could have handled the dog with greater gentleness. Yet, as Alex probed Kim's inside the tears were pouring down my face. Every moment Kim's suffering became more intolerable.

Portrait of Sir Timothy as an old dog

Alex gave a sigh of relief. 'I've got it.' He held up a sharp bone, about an inch long. 'It's all right boy. All over now . . . Lucky the bone's worked its way down. Let's hope it hasn't done any damage.'

'He have refused his food if it had,' I said, hopefully.

'Well, we'll see.'

We saw Sir Timothy shake himself from head to tail — the exuberant, sensuous shake of his young days. We watched him put away his dinner with undiminished appetite.

That night I did not have to carry him upstairs. He insisted on climbing up by himself — wearily, but with typical dachshund stubbornness. I knew that he would be with us to meet Ilit at London Airport.

'He's made it,' said Alex. 'Oh, I don't mean the stairs . . . Your bed. Make no mistake, that's where he's going to sleep in future. It's been the ambition of his life.'

FROM PLUTARCH'S *MORALIA*
Translated from the Greek by John Phillips, Gentleman, A.D. 1698

And indeed it is not easy to find out the natural Dexterity of any one ingenious and docible Animal, which is not accompany'd with more than one single Virtue.

Thus there is Affection towards their young ones, there is Desire of Praise. Where there is Generosity, there is also Moderation of Anger. Cunning likewise and Understanding are rarely parted from daring Boldness and Fortitude.

But as for those that rather chuse to divide and distinguish every one of these Virtues particularly by themselves, they shall find in Dogs a fair Demonstration of a gentle and yet lofty Mind at the same Time . . .

(The Philosopher Plutarch was born A.D. 46 at Chaeronea, Boeotia.)